Ladies' Night

Ladies' Night

Jack Ketchum

Gauntlet Publications
■ *2000* ■

Mass Market Trade Paperback ISBN 1-887368-35-3

Copyright © 1997/2000 by Dallas Mayr

Cover art copyright © 1997/2000 by Neal McPheeters

First printed by Silver Slamander Press in 1997

Manufactured in the United States of America

**FIRST MASS MARKET
TRADE PAPERBACK EDITION**

Gauntlet Publications
309 Powell Road, Springfield, PA 19064
Phone: (610) 328-5476
email: gauntlet66@aol.com
Website: http://www.gauntletpress.com

This one's for Paula White —
usually a lady but not always.

And for Richard Christenson,
who labored well and mightily.

"I deserve this fate. It's a debt I owe for a wild
and reckless life. So long, boys!"
— Bill Longley
hanged in Giddings, Texas, 1877

"If I'd the courage I would make my way home.
Too many antics in the forbidden zone."
— Adam and the Ants

"In the war between men and women
there are no survivors."
— Norman Mailer

Introduction

Truly attentive readers of mine, I mean real out-and-out detail-type-persons, may have noted that between 1981, when I published my first book, *Off Season,* and 1984, when I published my second — a little one-hundred-ninety-four-page thing called *Hide and Seek* — there was not a peep out of Jack Ketchum anywhere. No magazine work. No short stories. Nothing. And you might have asked yourself, so what in hell was this guy doing for three years? Sitting back counting his bucks?

I wish.

A good part of that time I was writing the novel you now have in hand. And writing it massively.

Plus privately I was scared as hell. Both during the writing and after.

To explain I have to backtrack some.

When Ballantine bought *Off Season* it created a lot of inhouse buzz precisely because it was so ferocious. In 1980 nobody had seen a book with quite so many teeth. That this was eventually to be its downfall had not yet occurred to anybody. But practically the whole damn house had read the book. I'd be walking with my editor and people would peer out at me from their cubicles, smiling and shaking their heads. This is the guy who wrote that crazy fucking thing about the cannibals. Marc Jaffe, who'd bought the novel, his first purchase as the new editor-in-chief there, took me aside one day and said, this book is going to make you rich, son.

Uh-huh.

I've written about all this before so I'll be brief. What happened in a nutshell was that they decided to mount this whole big campaign, posters and point-of-purchase display stands and an edition of 40,000 copies just for distributors, trying to advance-hype the thing — and the reaction of said distributors almost to a man was, excuse me? This shit is violent pornography and we want no part of it. Are you guys nuts?

But by the time they weighed in with that bad news I'd already contracted for a second book.

In January of '81 I signed to do a novel called *The Mantis Syndrome*. The title will become obvious to you once you've read the book. I changed it only because I liked the double entendre of *Ladies' Night* and *Mantis Syndrome* seemed just a little too Michael Crichton to me. I'd slaved over the outline and sample chapters — so much so that I've vowed never to do it again. The outline came to about forty pages. The chapters another forty. And then in writing the book I followed that outline just as slavishly.

I'll never do that again either.

Why did I put myself through all this? Because basically I was a little terrified.

Patti Smith once said something to the effect that they give you twenty-one years to produce your first album and six months to produce your second. She knows whereof she speaks. The idea for *Mantis* from a publishing standpoint was that the book was to be of the same flesh as *Off Season*, only bigger. Sort of my *'Salem's Lot* to *Off Season's Carrie*. Only Ketchum-style, with all the violence right in your face. This was, remember, months before the shit hit the fan with the distributors.

Ladies' Night

The advance was to be $20,000.00. Twice the advance for *Off Season* and very nice money in those days for a second novel. In fact it's very nice money these days but that's another story. I was still hearing all this buzz about the first book, how it was going to make a huge splash and how they had even bigger hopes for the second, I mean I was gonna be launched, friends. So there was plenty of pressure to top myself with this one.

And I had Patti's proverbial six months to do so. Literally.

I brought it in under the deadline, though. I worked long hours and followed the outline scrupulously because that was the outline Ballantine had bought. Scared every minute that I wouldn't pass muster, that I had only a few licks as a writer and that I'd used them all up in *Off Season*.

I've later learned this feeling's common. The I-Only-Have-One-Book-In-Me complex. I wish I knew it then.

But I brought it in and I brought it in big — over four hundred pages. That's right, the book before you once had a very serious case of elephantitis: I had explanatory subplots involving the military and science communities and another about a gay friend of my lead character's and his lover, I had fake newspaper articles and TV reports — I had all kindsa stuff. To date it's still the biggest book I've ever written. I had yet to learn for sure that less is sometimes more though I should have learned that from *Off Season*.

My only excuse — and it's a poor one — is that I was scared again. Ballantine wanted big and that's what I needed to deliver. Accent the word needed. Hence my first and only doorstop.

That wasn't what bothered Ballantine, though. They didn't seem to mind the bloating one bit. Does this surprise you? They're mass-market publishers for godsakes.

It was the violence, naturally.

By then the votes were in from the distributors. I could now walk through their 50th Street offices and almost hear the collective whoops. I got a two-page letter from my line-editor Susan Allison making lots of suggestions about how to bloat the book further and the only mention of cutting was, "we agreed that much of the violence must be taken out or held back. The story works very well without the gore." I say piffle. When you finish the book let's see what you think.

I didn't want to do the revisions. I don't think I was being arrogant about it. I was probably still too worried to be arrogant. It wasn't just cutting the violence either. Among other things they wanted to throw the whole story into the future and despite the science-fictiony premise this was decidedly not science fiction, this was horror, and the notion of imagining New York City ten or a hundred year from now held no appeal whatever. With a few exceptions I'd rarely even read science fiction. So while I dickered with Ballantine my agent at the time, Jack Scovil, quietly auctioned the book to pretty much every paperback company in town.

Stealth and cunning. It's an agent's job.

But we got no takers. Everybody was offended by the violence, particular the female editors, who thought I was misogynist in the extreme. One editor who shall remain nameless was kind enough to enclose her reader's report by mistake along with her rejection letter. I kept it. The report said, "I stopped reading every pearly word after the girls who work at the Burger King threw the would be (sic) hold-up man on the grill." Actually it's McDonald's. And the incident occurs only about a third of the way through so he or she didn't read much. Which is probably all to the good because considering what follows that scene's pretty mild. But the reader went on to conclude, "I hope the person who wrote this confines his aggressions to the page. This is pretty dreadful."

Words to live by.

The bottom line is, we never did sell it. Jack argued that I'd delivered an acceptable manuscript, which had followed the outline in every way. An understatement. And since it wasn't the writing — as I'd feared — it was the whole idea that bothered them at this point, I got to hold onto the advance. Ballantine sweetened the pot slightly in a contract for a third novel, the only caveat being that I was to hold down the bloodshed level on this one.

Jack's a pretty good agent.

Trouble was, for a long time I couldn't write the book. I was a one-book writer. The failure of *Ladies' Night* proved it. I was convinced.

Ladies' Night

I'd used up all my juice on the first book just as I'd suspected. Neither my agent nor the woman I lived with nor any of my friends who read and liked the book could talk me out of it. I could see myself going back to magazine work or a steady job, a fate too awful to conceive for anyone who has seen The Other Side. It was a crisis of confidence that lasted long and worked its way deep.

I spent a lot of time staying out late and getting up woozy in the morning. I was becoming Tom in *Ladies' Night*.

Then one day I got an idea for a small book, which would be written in the first person. I was re-reading James M. Cain at the time and thought, what if I do something like Cain does, draw characters who are in way over their heads and don't know it — only do it with a bunch of kids, teenagers. In the first person I'd have to break through and find some new licks.

Hide And Seek emerged. Crisis over.

But I could never really quit on *Ladies' Night*. Looking back I still liked the damn thing, thought the premise pretty audacious. But I kept it in a drawer and went on to other things until 1988. That year my old friend Richard Christenson — a playwright — and I were sitting in a bar one night and he was bemoaning quite rightly how difficult it was to make a buck in the business of writing drama, almost as tough as it was to make a buck in poetry, hell you might as well have been trying to sell pet roaches in this city and I found myself urging him to try some prose instead. I wasn't getting rich here but I was still afloat, doing what I wanted to do. Maybe so could he. As we talked it became clear he was game. I said here's an idea, why don't you see what you can do to trim some of the fat off *Ladies' Night,* whip it into shape and make it salable. We'll split the credit and the money fifty-fifty.

He spent months on the book, adding here, subtracting there, mostly subtracting — again to no avail. He did a partial rewrite of about the first quarter of the book and by the time he was finished I thought it was a wholly viable new take on it so we attached a far less gargantuan outline and Alice Martell, my agent by then, sent it out again.

All new editors, same responses.

Too violent. Too nasty toward women.

Personally I think it's just as nasty toward men. But maybe that's just me.

Anyway, once more I let it lie for awhile. In 1990 I decided to try a screenplay version. Thinking low-budget horror-movie I switched the locale from New York City to the suburbs to make for a far cheaper shoot but kept the mayhem basically the same. That script's still being shopped around now and then and I figure you never know. Especially with this yarn. Its voyage has been a long one.

Finally a couple of years ago I was between ideas for a new book, lying fallow, collecting this and that notion and waiting patiently for some pattern to emerge and thought, how about taking a slash-and-burn run at *Ladies' Night* in the meantime? Why not? Might be fun.

And it was. Trimmed by well over half its pages it closely resembled its sister-book, *Off Season.* It had the same simulated "real-time" timescale and worked like a well-made play, everything going on within the course of a single grisly night. It had the same theme of ordinary people being pushed to extraordinary acts of violence. Like *Off Season* its protagonists are not necessarily the nicest of people — Tom's a philanderer and morally something of a coward while Elizabeth's seriously thinking about fucking him, even though his wife's a friend and she baby-sits his son — the point being that nobody deserves to be pushed to these extremes, not ever.

Like the first book it steals liberally from the movies I happen to love, particularly — again like its predecessor — from *Night of the Living Dead.* Though this time the most obvious influence is David Cronenberg's first full-length feature, *Shivers,* aka *They Came From Within.*

I proceeded not from Richard's version but from the original, although many of the cuts I made were cuts he and I agreed were absolutely necessary — and I'm very much indebted to him for his fine eye and ear. Richard's version, I felt, had tried to explain too much of the science and its tone was more measured and serious than necessary for what was essentially just goofy pulp-horror fiction. I didn't want to be distracted by that. I wanted cheap thrills, period.

Hey, this is basically a story about some guy trying to get home after a really bad night at his local bar.

We've all had them.

The fact that it's also jabbing at the un-stuck nuclear family and male/female relationships in general's just gravy. It's there if you want it on your plate and practically unnecessary if you don't.

So I've kept the pulpy style, all the italics, all the exclamations, even some of my less successful sentence constructions for the sake of being true to the feel of the original and all the gore-hound excesses. In recent years I've tried for some slight measure of subtlety, some nuance of character and language, a few grace notes now and then. This has all the subtlety of a hooker selling blowjobs at the entrance to Lincoln Tunnel but I figure that's the way it should be.

Since I wrote the book times have changed — enough so that, happily for me, there are a few venues now for a story as extreme as this and you're looking at one of them.

Thanks, John.

But New York has changed too and probably will have changed again by the time you read this. "People come and go so quickly here," is as true of the Big Apple as it is of Oz. Only it's businesses that disappear overnight here, with new ones flinging themselves all tarted up in the morning. Bars, florists, banks, everything. If you're a native New Yorker and especially if you know the West Side you're going to note discrepancies in the novel as to setting. I've updated the neighborhood wherever I could, replacing a bank with, say, HMV Music if that's what's there today. But in some cases that wasn't possible. The butcher shop on Broadway, for instance, is long gone and long lamented. But I needed a butcher shop so I kept it. Author privilege. To do otherwise would be to write a whole new novel, not polish up and older one.

Hollywood's a funny place. You write a screenplay, you go out there and you spend a whole lot more time pitching it than you did in the writing of it or than anybody will ever spend in the reading. Everyone seems to want you to come up with the gist of the thing in a single pithy line, like a sky-hook from which they can suspend their thoughts about what to do or what not to do about "the project." To buy or not to buy. To amend or not to amend — or rather just what to amend. Casting, money, shooting schedule, everything. It all seems to hang on that hook, depend on that line. So I came up with the hook for *Ladies' Night.*

I had to. *Ladies' Night* was the one that simply would not go away.

Think I'll leave you with that hook and then let you get on to the novel. Like the book itself I still kinda like the feel of it.

"In the war between men and women, the shooting has begun."

Pow.

Sweets

If you could make an arrest for bad temper, thought Lederer, this whole damn city would be on Rikers Island.

He stepped off the curb into the street. Horns blared behind him. The uniforms had blocked off Riverside from 72nd up to 75th and the diversion onto Broadway was causing an angry tangle. He'd parked on Columbus and walked over. It was easier.

The warm wind gusting off the river tugged at his hat.

The stink was powerful. Sweet. Cloying. He could not say what it reminded him of. But something.

The tanker lay like a huge cracked egg frying in the middle of the street, its spill a great wide slick of dark thick liquid pooling from the center line out along the western curb.

He stepped carefully around it.

A white Buick wagon lay sprawled on its side at the corner of 73rd. There was very little left of its rear compartment. The windshield was shattered on the driver's side and spackled with blood.

He could pretty much guess what happened. The Buick had turned onto Riverside against the light. The trucker was moving fast and hit his brakes to avoid it. Much too late and much too hard.

They were tricky, these tankers. Especially if you ran them full and without baffles, the heavy sheets of steel which lay inside the tank, separating the load into compartments so that they took some of the wave-action when you braked. Without the baffles you could still brake fast if you had to. But you'd better not turn the wheel. Because if you did you had maybe 9,500 gallons behind you and all this weight, this huge wave of liquid back there starts to push forward, jack-knifing the cab at the fifth wheel and ramming you with every bit of its weight like a battering ram.

You had to be one hell of a driver to control all that. He guessed this one wasn't.

There wasn't much left of him.

Again it was easy to imagine. The tank had jack-knifed the cab all the way around to what was probably no more than a ten degree angle. Then the wave effect started. The first wave went forward, the second back, and the third side-to-side — all of it one great heaving surge of motion. It was the side-to-side that killed the driver — toppling the tank off its sub-frame directly onto his cab, squashing it like a card-board container. The man inside was nothing but a wide smear of red and grey between the crushed roof and the fake-leather seat. A bug against a windshield.

It had been fast, anyway.

The guy had that much luck.

McCann was standing by the traffic light. He walked over.

"What's the cargo?" Lederer asked.

"Damned if I know. Smells sweet. Liquid sweetener or something. Take a look at the logo there."

Painted in red letters along the side of the tank were the words LADIES, INC.

"What the hell's that mean?" said Lederer.

McCann shrugged. "I guess it means that at least we can assume our feet won't glow in the dark."

Lederer lit a cigarette and watched the cleanup crew work the spill and the wrecking crew try to pull fifty-five feet of steel off the guy in the cab.

Uniforms held the perimeter. A good-sized crowd had gathered. Some were standing on park benches. A few kids mostly — were perched in trees, looking for a better view. It would take a while but they'd get their view all right, when the boys pulled off that tank.

"What about the wagon?"

"Woman in the driver's seat, no passengers. Mid-twenties I'd say. No seatbelt. My wife does the same thing. I tell her, use the goddamn seatbelt but she knows better. And me out here looking at this shit a dozen times a month. They took her down to Roosevelt half an hour ago. You ask me, she's not going to make it."

The wind was up now, blowing west to southeast off the river, and Lederer thought I ought to get those kids out of the trees. A little gusting, a few more miles-per-hour and they could get into some trouble up there. Riverside Park, with its thin dark soil and macadam walkways, was a hard place to fall.

"I don't get it," he said. "What the hell was a tanker even doing here?" He pointed to the sign on the streetlight behind them. "Look at that. This whole damn street is posted. Not just here, but back at the corner of 72nd and Broadway and again right there at the entrance to Riverside. NO COMMERCIAL TRAFFIC. Every couple of blocks. Plus he had to be really moving to do that much damage to the Buick. So what the hell was he doing in the first place, highballing it through Manhattan?"

"Maybe we got a driver who can't read," said McCann.

"No way. You can't read you don't move freight. He knew where he was going. He knew it was illegal. He did it anyway."

"The route-sheet in the cab," said McCann. "Maybe we'll get it there."

"Maybe."

But he had a feeling that the only thing they'd find in the cab was a messy driver. Without documentation. Beneath the sickly-sweet scent of the cargo he thought he detected another smell — the stink of greed and corruption.

The usual.

Cut corners, cover-ups. The cheap shot at the fast buck. The city was made of that. More and more that was what it was all about these days as the economy and government and the whole damn shooting match seemed to wind down slowly into disaster.

Naturally there were victims. A young woman in a white Buick.

One wrong turn and it all came hurtling down at you.

He watched the progress of the wrecking crew. At this rate it would be hours before they could pry the tank away. In the meantime it would probably be a good idea to talk with the boys in the lab. Find out what this stuff was. Check the plates on the tanker. A company registration, maybe, for LADIES, INC. Punch it up on the computer.

"Listen," he said to McCann, "if anything breaks you call me, okay?"

"Sure."

"Especially on that route-sheet."

"Will do."

Lederer crossed the street, headed back to his car. It was 2:30 in the afternoon and the day was hot — hot and humid even with the breeze, ennervating — and he suddenly had the feeling there was going to be a whole lot of work to do before his shift was over.

Halfway down Columbus it hit him.

The smell.

It was weaker here, weak enough so that he could finally get a handle on it — something specific and not just a too-sweet reek. It made no sense. But what it reminded him of filled him with a kind of strange elation.

Cherry, he thought.

Cherry lollipops, to be more exact. That good bright artificial smell he remembered liking so much as a kid, wafting along on a westerly breeze. Cherry-flavored lollipops.

His favorite kind.

Breezing the Apple

The winds were island winds swirling off the Hudson.

At Riverside park a small black boy climbed out of the trees and chased his baseball cap through the gutter as it tumbled away. At Lincoln Center in front of Avery Fisher Hall a fashion model returning home from another round of go-sees stepped into a tiny whirlwind of swirling city debris and felt a speck of grit lodge itself beneath her green-tinted contact lens. In mid-town a stack of the New York Times tugged at its paperweight, inching it off-center.

The winds coursed through the wide city streets, swept upwards in a sudden rush against skyscrapers and highrises to disperse slowly into the calmer air above. By far the winds blew strongest west to southeast — the cool ocean breeze out of the east stopped them dead, forcing steel-and-concrete superheated air up to the cloudless sky like an uppercut to the chin of a boxer. Random currents reached eastward into the 80's and slid south down through the Village and Soho, though much diffused in power.

But mostly they poured through the open mouth of the west of Manhattan, down Riverside, down Columbus and Amsterdam, down Broadway, until other currents scattered them, eviscerating their inland thrust.

North as far as West 86th Street, south as far as 39th, east to Central Park and in pockets beyond, Manhattanites, tourists, and bus-and-tunnel commuters to New Jersey, Westchester, Long Island and Connecticut could be seen to pause a moment to sniff the air as something rushed by them and then darted swiftly on, something sweet, redolent of memories of near or distant pasts, of sunny summer days much like this one, when their worlds were simpler, easier.

Before the world and they grew old.

Party On the Roof

"What you missed," Susan was saying, "was the security strike."

Tom Braun looked at his wife and then at Elizabeth and thought, I've probably got the two most attractive women in the building standing here — so why do I feel like I need a real drink?

"It was actually fun in a way," said Susan. "They had no other choice but to enlist the tenants so Tom and I sat desk-duty four nights running. You'd be amazed at what goes on around here."

Elizabeth smiled. "Tell."

Susan looked around to see if anyone was in listening range. She needn't have bothered. The party was winding down now, the food mostly gone and the wine running low, only twenty-five or thirty of them left up there on the rooftop, their laughter and conversation fading back into the noise from the street twenty-two stories below, into the warm evening breeze.

It was one of those amazing summer evenings where it almost would have taken an act of will to have kept him indoors. The day's humidity had finally given way. Had the Dorset Towers Tenants' Association decided to hold their party elsewhere — in the lobby or someone's apartment — he would have stayed home.

"Well, the Landrus feed their daughter Prozak, for one thing."

"You're kidding."

"Risley lives next door. It seems that little Carla has this habit of running away nights, nobody knows where. One night last month the police got involved, brought her home drunk at three in the morning. Risley says there was quite a commotion in the hall, with everybody hurling guilt at one another. Of course he listened carefully to the whole thing. And you know Sam Hardin, don't you?"

"The doctor? The old retired guy who hangs around the mailroom all day?"

"Uh-huh."

Elizabeth shuddered. "I know him. He stares at you," she said. "He's creepy."

"Okay, follow this. You know Dan, the doorman?"

She pointed to the rooftop entrance. Some of the security staff were standing there talking next to a starved potted plant. Dan — a tall good-looking black man — was among them. Elizabeth nodded.

"Well, Dan has something going with Eleanor Snow — you didn't know that? Oh yeah, for quite a while now. Anyway according to Eleanor, Dan says old Sam apparently likes a good hard thrashing now and then — hires expensive hookers who bring along suitcases full of equipment. I guess the girls look okay, because management hasn't complained yet, but the whole desk staff knows who they are and why they're there. The problem is Sam's getting kind of loud about it. The neighbors are getting nervous."

"I love it," said Elizabeth. "Perversion!"

"*No, Crossfire* is perversion," said Tom. "Sam's just kinky."

"You two are turning into a pair of old gossips, you know that?"

"Yeah," said Tom. "It's good the strike didn't last much longer. Real-life neighborhood soaps can hook you."

He watched Susan sip her wine and thought how different these two women were. It wasn't just the disparity in their ages. His wife made even the plastic wineglass in her hand look elegant. She had that way about her. A cool natural WASP patrician style. This despite that fact that in reality the former Susan Ackerman ran the drama research department over at the Lincoln Center Library for the Performing Arts — a librarian — an important but distinctly unglamourous job where what counted was smarts and efficiency, not style.

Whereas Elizabeth looked exactly like what she was — a twenty-year-old singer-slash-dancer-slash-actress who would always be far more at home on a stage with a top hat and tails than standing around sipping sherry.

Maybe that was what he found so damned attractive about her. That straightforwardness.

Jesus, he thought. You're thirty-nine. She's twenty.

Grow up.

He had to admit, though, that having her home again after two months out in L. A. already was making him nervous.

He watched Mr. and Mrs. Daniels walk slowly by arm in arm and smile at them.

"You're not leaving?" Susan said.

"Oh yes, dear," said Mrs. Daniels. "It's well past our dinner time." Her husband patted one liver-spotted arm.

"Have a lovely evening," said Susan.

"I believe we will. You too, dear. All of you."

They disappeared through the doorway.

"You know what she told me?" Susan said.

"What?" said Elizabeth.

"Tonight's their thirtieth wedding anniversary. And can you believe it? She's cooking. Something special, she said. Just for him."

"That's sweet."

"They're nice people. I look at them and they always seem so happy together. They really still seem to be in love with one another."

"It happens," said Tom. Damned infrequently.

The crowd had thinned by now. He recognized most of them but knew only a few by name. Risley was still there. The dark sallow businessman was talking to a pretty blonde girl near the Broadway side of the rooftop. The girl was half his age. Risley did pretty well supposedly and Tom could never figure why. There was something unctuous about the man despite his apparent friendliness, something Tom disliked instinctively.

Maybe you're just jealous, he thought.

He watched another girl move past them and for a moment caught her eye, a dark thin girl in a pale yellow dress who he recognized as another dancer — this close to Lincoln Center there were a lot of them in the building. He remembered her saying that she studied at ABT. He'd spoken to her once in the laundry room on the second floor. She'd been open and friendly.

Now she frosted him as though he were a stranger.

He felt rebuffed.

For what he didn't know.

"How was the flight?" he asked Elizabeth.

She sighed. "Grueling. We were two hours late out of LAX. I haven't even unpacked yet. But it was too nice an evening to stay indoors. I had a glass of flat ginger ale and sat staring at my bags for a few minutes and said to hell with it and came on up."

"It is a beautiful evening," said Susan.

He had to agree. The sun lay low on the horizon yet already the moon was out. Bright streaks of red and gold on one side and the grey-white moon on the other. It was going to be clear tonight. Even in New York you'd be able to see the stars.

"The moon's full," said Tom. "Summer madness."

"Sure," said Elizabeth.

"It's true. I did a piece on it for *Parade* once. Years ago. While I was still — you know — writing. Twice a day the ocean rises and falls about four feet I think it is, pulled by the moon's gravity. We're seventy-five percent water so it pulls us too. The pull's greatest at full moon and new moon. And so is emergency-room activity. Assaults, rapes, suicides. That kind of thing. They've computerized the police statistics and there really is a correspondence. Plus any nurse will tell you that there are a lot more babies born when the moon's full. Stirs the hormones or something."

"I remember that piece," said Susan. "Aren't we supposed to lose about a 100th of a gram of weight, something like that?"

"The full-moon diet!" said Elizabeth. They laughed.

"Hey" said Tom. "The moon's a woman. And women do like their diets."

They ignored that.

"I never thought it was fair," said Susan. "The sun's always a man and the moon's always a woman, in just about every culture. Take Diana. She's goddess of the hunt and the moon. Why that combination I don't know. Maybe because we were nighthunters first, skulking around the savannahs by moonlight. Or men were, anyhow, I dunno. But it's Apollo — her brother — who brings light and prosperity. You ever hear of a man bringing light and prosperity?"

"Edison. But not recently," Tom agreed.

"I really do think there's something to this tidal pull business, though" said Elizabeth. "I'm not much for the bars god knows but it seems like every time I sort of get restless at night and want to go out, I look up at the sky and there it is. A full moon."

"Same here," said Tom.

Susan gave him a look. She didn't like him hitting the bars, moon or no moon. And she certainly didn't appreciate his mentioning this particular form of recreation to Elizabeth.

Fuck it, he thought. I do what I do. Damned if I'm hiding anything.

"How's Andy?" said Elizabeth. Changing the subject. Susan's early frost had not been lost on her. A bright young lady.

"Andy's fine," she said. "His head-cold's gone and neither of us caught it for a change. He and Matt Donovan are off to see some ridiculous horror movie called *Coven*. I think he missed you, though. You should drop by and see him tomorrow."

"I will."

It was then that he saw the dancer again.

And heard the strange low moan all the way across the rooftop.

Heads were turning.

He saw her crouched against the four-foot concrete retaining wall. There was something in her hands but Risley and the blonde were in the way so that at first he couldn't see. Then what remained of the crowd parted — he could almost feel a wave of shocked revulsion coming off them as they moved away — and then he could see, and instantly wished he hadn't.

She had a half-empty litre bottle of wine. She was holding it in both hands and moving it back and forth beneath the light yellow dress.

Moving it inside her.

Her eyes were rolling, her teeth clenched and she trembled, moaning.

Her lips pulled away from grinding teeth, sweat poured off her face, her long hair thrashing.

The hem of the dress was stained with blood.

"Jesus!"

"Let me by," somebody said behind him. "I'm a doctor."

Tom watched the old man move through the crowd. He was aware of Dan and another security man, Gonzales, standing next to him and Susan.

The girl was pushing deeper. Blood was running down both her legs.

The old man reached for the bottle.

"It's all right," he said gently. "Easy now. Give me the bottle. Come on."

Her eyes flashed open.

Her mouth twisted.

The doctor had a single sudden moment to recognize his danger and Tom saw him stagger, unbelieving, as the base of the bottle slammed against his chin, its force enormous, the bottle shattering and continuing upward in a bloody arc across his face and forehead.

Dan was already moving. Gonzales a step behind him.

The dancer dropped the broken bottleneck and turned to face the retaining wall.

Raised one leg and began to climb.

Dan lunged at her low, wrenched her off the wall, wrapped his arms around her legs while Gonzales grabbed her waist from the other side. The girl struggled, screaming, a high-pitched furious wail as she pounded Dan's head and shoulders. The black man kept his head down low, in what was almost a boxer's stance, and held on.

They hauled her flailing toward the door.

The doctor lay on his side trying to stop the pulse of blood with his hands and then his handkerchief. A wide flap of flesh depended from his chin. He kept trying to hold it in place. Residents were coming to his aid.

Now that she was out of there.

At the doorway the girl grabbed hold of the casing trim, resisting with all her might. Two big men, he thought, and they can barely move her. Her mouth spewed foam, spittle flying as she struggled. Two more security guards appeared on either side, began to pry her fingers off the trim one by one. She screamed and tried to bite, lurching like a snapping dog.

The fingers lost their purchase.

Stumbling on the staircase they hauled her down.

The door slammed shut behind them.

The screams from below faded. They had got her into the elevator and were on their way down.

Drugs, someone murmured.

Crazy.

She always seemed like such a nice girl.

Risley and Bob Hobart were helping the doctor to the door. The doctor had all he could do to keep his bloodsoaked handkerchief pressed against his face and keep from fainting. Risley and Hobart practically had to carry him.

Guests were leaving. Among those who stayed behind a hush had fallen and the cheap wine was suddenly popular again.

"What the hell was that?" said Elizabeth.

"Damned if I know."

"Let's go," said Susan.

They walked out the exit door, down the short flight of stairs and through the hall to the bank of elevators. Tom pressed the call button. They stood together waiting in a strange vivified silence.

The double doors opened and they stepped inside. Tom hit number 2. Susan leaned heavily against the wall. No one spoke. The elevator slid seamlessly down the twenty stories to their floor and stopped.

They stepped out into the long, dimly-lit hallway.

Outside, it was not yet dark.

The Island of Dr. Moreau

There was no escaping the voices once they started.

Some nights he'd lie here with a pillow over his head but it didn't help, he kept listening, despite himself — *trying* to hear, almost, which was weird because he sure didn't want to — and even if most of it was just a muffled blur things still got through, especially his name, especially that, especially when they said *Andy.* And his name came up a lot.

His Walkman was busted and he'd lost his tv and Sega Genesis privileges for a week over that shouting-in-class thing *(how come it was okay for them to shout but not for him?)* so that left reading. Sometimes he could pick up a book or an old copy of *Eerie* or *Creepy* or *Vampirella* and read until their voices were just a dull droning in his head, until the stories got, to him. Maybe he could do that now.

He was at the part in *The Island of Dr. Moreau* where Pendrick goes to the Beast People and hears the Saying of the Law. Maybe that would do it.

He could hear them in the living room yelling about Lizzy. He heard her name. Elizabeth this. Elizabeth that. Something about his dad and women. He didn't know if his dad went out with other women though he knew he did go out alone nights sometimes — but what Lizzy would have to do with that he didn't know and didn't like to think about.

Lizzy was okay. He liked Lizzy a lot. He didn't care what his mom was saying. She treated him like a person, not like some stupid kid. She hardly ever yelled. She didn't like horror movies much but she did like movies, even the action stuff. They'd pick up stuff at Tower Video together and never argued about what to rent. Lizzy wasn't just a sitter, she was a friend.

He wondered what would happen if he just walked in there and told them to please shut up.

He thought he knew what the answer to that would be.

So if you couldn't do that then what *did* you do?

You sat there. You sat there in your room wishing they were happier, wishing they didn't have to fight so much or that even if they did fight you didn't have to hear it and feel bad for some dumb reason, as though it were your fault, as though they'd been happy before you came along and screwed things up for them. His dad said they were *always* happy at first. Did that mean they'd started to get mad at one another before they had him or only after?

He'd wondered that a lot. But he couldn't really ask them. Because what if they said *after?* Nobody was going to say, you rotten kid, it's your fault. No matter what the truth was they'd try to make it sound like he had nothing to do with it. But he'd know. He'd know and then what would he do?

He rolled over on his back and stared up at the ceiling.

He was glad he'd be going to camp in a week or two. He had all his gear ready in the closet — canteen, scout knife, and a forty-pound bow with a quiver full of target arrows. His mom hadn't liked the bow and arrows but his dad had had one as a kid and sided with him for a change. Camp was probably stupid basically and it wasn't that he loved the woods — in fact he was a little scared of sleeping out there — but at least he'd be out of this place, away from this awful aching worrying and caring and this anger whenever they got to doing this.

Ladies' Night

He reached for his copy of *The Island of Dr. Moreau* and started reading.

"Are we not men?" said the Swine Men and the Leopard Men.

Misshapen and forlorn, they ambled him through the dark island forest.

Ladies On the Second Floor

She was almost finished stacking the dishwasher when the phone rang in the hall. Her headache was a killer. The sound of running water, clattering plates, and now the telephone, didn't help any.

"Tom? Can you get it, please?"

Tension and cheap wine, she thought. I ought to know better. The phone continued ringing.

She could hear CNN in the living room.

He wasn't moving.

She turned off the water, grabbed a hand-towel and walked into the living room. Tom was sitting in the easy chair scowling at the tv screen. She walked past him to the hall and the phone rang again as she reached for the receiver.

"Hello?"

No one answered.

Now what the hell was this? One of his goddamn girlfriends? She did hear breathing. Only it wasn't the usual obscene-caller breathing. It was lighter, softer.

Like a woman's.

"Who is this?"

When the woman spoke she could barely hear her.

"Saint Luke's hospital? I need . . . I need . . ."

My god. *That again,* she thought. The woman was one digit off. It was a six instead of a seven in the fifth number you dialed. Once when they'd been living over on 72nd Street it had been the Ginko Gardens. A Chinese restaurant. That was one digit off in the seventh number. She didn't know which was worse, people phoning for take-out or the sad, troubled voices that sometimes called for the hospital.

Like this one.

The woman sounded bad.

"Sorry, you've got the wrong number. You want 397-0644."

". . . could you, please . . ."

Pleading with her.

"I'm sorry."

She hung up.

It wasn't nice to do that just like that but the headache was describing intricate whirls of pain inside her skull and there was a misery in the woman's voice, almost a panic, that she simply couldn't handle. Let her dial it again, she thought. She'll get through.

She walked back into the living room.

"Thanks," she said.

He didn't even look at her.

It was always this way after a fight. One or the other of them simply stopped talking. She was as bad as he was.

It hadn't always been this way.

There was a time they'd talked things through. Before the affairs started. Before he started drinking. Before he'd quit his job at the agency with the ridiculous idea that he could write a novel.

The ridiculous idea that he could *sell* a novel. Because he'd written one, all right. A *literary* novel. It went on and on for about five hundred pages. Taking the high road to nowhere.

A novel just wasn't in him.

So he'd gone back to work as an editor, hating it. Hating himself for that matter — she knew that — but unlike her he refused to try therapy, which was what he really needed.

The drinking was compulsive.

He didn't realize it but Tom was on the run from her. And from Andy. He had been for a while now. Ties to home and family were not so much ties as a long leash. He tugged at it constantly.

And unless things changed it was only a matter of time before he left them altogether.

There was nothing she could do about it.

She had come to realize that with a growing sadness.

She started back to the kitchen.

"I'm going out," he said.

She thought, *now why doesn't that surprise me?*

She wanted to cry. The headache was raging.

"All right."

She stood there a moment in case there was more.

There wasn't.

She decided to let the dishes go for a while. She needed to lie down. The Tylenol with codeine hadn't kicked in. The headache was growing roots in her head. Maybe some aspirin.

On the way to the bathroom she passed Andy's room and thought, thank god you'll be in camp soon. At first she'd been against his going. For purely selfish reasons. She knew how much she'd miss him.

But Andy didn't need this constant tension. It seemed to her that sending him to camp was yet another turning point in their relations, a kind of surrender. We can't quite accommodate you, Andy, it seemed to say, not the way we are now. We've tried to but we can't. I love you with all my heart but this has got to be worked out between us once and for all. So go off and at least for now, have a good time, have some fun — and maybe we'll screw you up that much less.

She closed the bathroom door behind her and looked at herself in the mirror.

You look like hell, she thought. There was a redness in her eyes as though she'd been crying. Her skin looked blotchy.

She opened the cabinet and reached for the aspirin. Behind the bottle she noticed Tom's old stained tortoise-shell straight razor. The razor had belonged to his father. Tom never used it and she'd have liked to throw it away especially with a child around but Tom had insisted. She couldn't argue. He had precious little left of his father.

She opened the bottle.

She heard the front door to their apartment open and then close again.

Not even a goodbye, she thought.

What the hell's happened to us?

She shook out two aspirin and swallowed them dry, recapped the bottle and returned it to the shelf. She closed the cabinet door and looked at herself again in the mirror.

I look old, she thought. I look old and tired and tense and . . .

. . . oh god I look ugly.

Suddenly and without warning she felt an overwhelming sadness and pressed her hands over her face to stifle the sob so that Andy wouldn't hear. There was a pressure in her chest that seemed at once to oppress her and flood her with adrenaline. It wrenched at her muscles and filled her eyes with tears. She felt dizzy and light-headed and thrust her hand out to steady herself and heard the mirror crack.

She looked up in surprise and drew her hand away. She saw that she'd been lucky — she wasn't cut. But the mirror was shattered, a silvery, crystalline spider-web that seemed to buckle inward.

My god, she thought. There's a quarter inch of glass on that mirror, backed with stainless steel.

She opened it carefully so as not to jar loose the broken glass and stared, barely comprehending. There was a dent the size of a baseball in the steel backing.

How could she be capable of that kind of impact?

She felt the urge to cry again.

God! get to *bed,* she thought. She carefully closed the cabinet door.

Weaving and unsteady she walked across the hall to the bedroom and slid into bed. She was frightened. It had come on so suddenly. From headache to . . . this. If she'd known where Tom was going she'd have called him.

Help. Just this once.

She closed her eyes and tried to relax into the pillow, to block everything out, all the events of the day that may have caused this sudden panic. But the tears kept coming, more quietly but unstoppable, and there was still this strange feeling inside her and this surging adrenaline.

She felt a slim thread of anger connect and tense the muscles of her body. It was alloyed with fear. The anger was specific, its focus Tom and Andy. At Tom for leaving her alone again. At Andy for being the locus and nexus of her guilt. The fear was more diffuse. It rose partly out of the anger, because she did not really know why the anger should be there. Certainly not when it came to Andy.

She loved Andy.

She could never hurt him.

But the thought was insistent.

She could crack them. Both of them. As easily as she'd cracked the mirror.

No!

Pressure bore down upon her like rough hands. She opened her eyes in apprehension, struggling for control. She felt a clutching between her legs, an ache, demanding. It connected somehow to Tom and Andy. Her eyes squinted shut and for a moment it was better that way. The empty darkness.

And then she saw that summer by the shore when she was a little girl and her mother had coaxed her into water that was too deep and her father was dying of cancer and she saw faces of friends she had lost touch with years ago, in college, in high school for god's sake, heard them accuse her of faithlessness, of never having loved them. She saw the moment of Andy's birth.

What in god's name is happening to me?

She was dying.

This was supposed to happen when you died, wasn't it? In the seconds before. Faces, a life remembered. But she knew she wasn't dying. She felt a deep, dreamlike restlessness — like a fever-dream, wakefulness and a kind of hypnogenetic sleep driving one another like a mingling of poison kisses. And now she was the object of hate and scorn, the scorn of complete strangers, people and shadow-images chasing her through a bright empty landscape as she ran from them with all her power. *Open your eyes,* she thought.

She did.

The room was gone.

The running, the strangers, the deep water, the friends who were no longer friends — all of them were still there.

Relax, she thought. Relax and sleep. Because this is all right if you're asleep. But if you're awake you're crazy. Breath deep. She closed her eyes.

The images engulfed her, a film running just behind her eyelids.

She submitted.

Eventually, after some time, her sense of desperation faded. The ache remained, and so did the fear and the anger but they were easier to bear now, less at odds with one another, part of a whole. She could open her eyes and the room was as it should be, back to normal — though she thought that she had never seen shadows so deeply formed and textured. But she preferred to keep them shut now. A man was running from her through the city streets. That, at least, made a kind of sense to her.

So that when it came at last and enveloped her completely she only thought, this is not exactly sleep, and sank slowly into a silent warren of dim nightmares and they did not unduly disturb her.

Outside the wind was rising. She felt it cool her cheeks.

It was her last real sensation.

She — Susan — wife to Tom and mother to Andy, protagonist for thirty-eight years to her own life story, began to disappear.

Elizabeth lay naked on her bed and felt the breeze from the big screened window drift gently over her body, damp with sweat against the fresh sheets. As always after exercising, her body felt tight and strong. The temperature tonight was perfect, cooling, soothing. She stretched, her muscles expanding and then relaxing, tendrils of summer wind reaching beneath her to the small of her back arched against the bedsheets.

She heard laughter outside the window. She got up and looked.

Ladies' Night

Tom Braun and Dan, the doorman.

As far as she was concerned, the two most attractive guys in the building.

That she was attracted to Dan vaguely pleased her. She'd never been turned on by a black man before and it was nice to know that it was possible. A kind of skewed racism, she supposed, but there you had it.

That she was attracted to Tom didn't please her one damn bit. She was younger than Tom and Susan by nearly twenty years but they were more than neighbors — she considered them friends. She considered Andy a friend too and here she was, more than a little interested in his father.

Not that she would ever do anything about it.

Not while he and Susan were together.

She watched him turn and walk away, headed east toward Broadway. Dan stood at the door, his smile gradually fading, looking out at the street, unaware of her naked in the window a floor above.

In L.A. during the shoot a low-budget thriller called *Hide and Seek* — her apartment had faced nothing more interesting than the generator. She had missed this one. She had missed watching the cabs pull up through the circular driveway to the three glass doors, the big black limos, watching people come and go, catching snatches of conversation and the sounds of traffic, the rain in the garden, the birch tree brushing against her window.

A second-floor front apartment in New York City. You had only to open a window to let the world inside.

On a still afternoon she could hear singing lessons being given somewhere above her, voices and a firm piano. Across the way a cellist practiced daily.

Sometimes she thought she heard gunfire — though they were probably just backfires. Even this she enjoyed since they held no threat to her directly. Along with the police sirens and fire engines wailing through the streets this was New York to her, its urgency, its drama.

It was good to be home.

Tom was the only problem. A problem she couldn't let *become* a problem.

There had been noises — shouting — coming from their kitchen earlier. She'd gone into her own kitchen for a cup of coffee and she could hear them faintly through the wall. That she could hear them at all meant they were pretty loud. Which meant they'd been fighting again.

She felt awful for Andy.

It wasn't fair. Half the men she met were absolute total fuck-ups and the other half were either gay or married. Same old song.

Tom was a nice man basically. She'd sensed that right away. Maybe not right now, maybe not to himself or Susan or even to Andy sometimes, but she sensed that once he got out of this particular job and into another that would change. A job you hated could turn everything sour.

A man like Tom was temptation.

Because . . . maybe . . . you only had to wait.

Go unpack, she thought. Get out of the window. Before somebody sees you up here stark naked and decides to climb a tree.

Instead of unpacking she sighed and rolled back onto the bed. She ran her hands slowly over the good firm flesh of her stomach. Her skin was dry by now and warm. She remembered that Susan and some of the others had been talking at the patty about smelling lollipops or something this afternoon — some kind of candy — asking if she'd smelled it too. But she was still in the air over Kennedy. She smiled mischievously.

If she had a lollipop now, she'd suck it.

Cut it out, she thought.

It was still early but it had been a long day. She was exhausted.

She closed her eyes and thoughts of Tom came unbidden while she listened to the sounds of the street and the city night. She moved a hand to her breast and felt it pulse with her heartbeat.

You can unpack tomorrow, she thought.

To hell with it.

A short time later she fell asleep.

Into the Nightlife

At the corner of 69th Street Tom waited while a black stretch limo went by, and then he crossed the street. The entrance to the Burnside — a high-rise much like his own — was busy at the moment, not just the usual tenants coming and going but couples lounging against the big red-brick planters and a steady flow of well-dressed yuppies moving through the revolving doors. Somebody was throwing a party.

He passed a furniture store and a lighting store, long-necked chromium lamps peering out through the windows like spacecraft from War *of the Worlds.* Across the street the vegetable market and butcher shop were still open and doing good business. The beauty parlor and Japanese restaurant next to them would probably fold with the next rent-hike.

On the center strip of fenced-in scraggly grass and trees that divided Broadway a drunk was doing a tap dance for the amusement of the passers-by.

He passed a drugstore, a Baskin-Robbins and a McDonald's. On the northwest corner of 71st Street in front of a bar two young cops were trying to pull a middle-aged woman into their cruiser. They couldn't seem to get hold of her. She kept flapping her arms like some huge gawky flightless bird. A crowd was gathering, smiling, laughing. Tom stopped for the light and watched them.

The woman's blue summer suit was expensive and so were the high-heel shoes. A Bloomingdales' bag sat beside her on the curb. At the moment she was using the shoes against the cops, trying to kick them where it would do the most good. So far they were managing to avoid her. Then she dropped the purse off her shoulder, swung it and hit the cop on her left full in the face.

Thwack.

Good leather.

"Shit!" said the cop and grabbed himself a fistful of summer suit, pulling her backward by the shoulder and forearm while his partner went for her thighs, lifting her off the ground. A homeless guy opened the back door of the prowl car for them with a flourish and they shoved her inside.

Summer in the City.

The woman was calling them every name in the book, banging on the windows, mad as hell. The cop she'd hit in the face climbed into the driver's seat while the other cop retrieved her Bloomie's bag and slid into the passenger side. They drove away.

He crossed 71st Street, passed a rollerblade shop, a jewelry store, a restaurant, a Photomat, a natural food store, and a vegetable market. At a kiosk at 72nd Street he bought himself a *Post* in case there was nothing doing at the bar and a pack of Winstons. The girl who ran the kiosk was very pretty, with long brown silky hair. He'd seen her there before and wondered how a woman that good-looking wound up in a street-peddler's job. He glanced at the headline of the *Post.*

16 DEAD IN LOVE-SUICIDE PACT.

He turned left on 72nd Street, wondering what the hell *that* was all about.

There were still a few cigar-chomping old men in front of the OTB discussing the day's action. The TV sets were still on in the window of

Ladies' Night

72nd Street Electronics, Murphy Brown hauling her new baby into the office on a dozen screens. Across the street the mannequins in Areil posed lubriciously in silk camisoles, negligees and lace bodysuits — bringing Elizabeth, similarly attired, right to mind.

Hands off, he thought. Both physically and mentally.

Enough. You've got enough problems as it is.

You bought into *her*, he thought. Into Susan. The problem is not Susan but that you're too damn young to have a family. You didn't buy into *them* and supporting them in a job you hated. Much as he loved Andy.

It felt too damn much like the end of things.

A light was still on in the mystery bookstore between the butcher shop and the travel agency. He'd worked in a bookstore once as a teenager one summer and knew the light on this late meant they were probably taking inventory inside.

Beside the bookstore was a fish market and beside the market was MacInery's.

Class, he thought.

His favorite bar was next to a fish store.

He peered through the plate-glass window. It looked pretty lively. Bailey was behind the bar and he recognized a few of the regulars. He saw that the women were out in pretty good number. MacInery's was a neighborhood place and women tended to feel comfortable there. So instead of the usual New York quota of, say, four guys to every woman, MacInery's ratio was more like two to one, and sometimes it was dead even. He folded his Post, tucked it under his arm and pushed open the door.

The jukebox blared. Bailey glanced up from behind the bar and smiled.

The crowd opened up for him like a mouth always hungry for more and he moved on inside.

The Westside

For a weekend summer night the streets were quiet.

At the World Cafe and the Aegean on Columbus and at the trendier China Club uptown at the Beacon Hotel on Broadway the crowds were still thin and would remain so until about midnight.

Further uptown, at Pearlie's on 84th Street, a young early drunk stumbled on his way out the door — but here the long narrow barspace was already so crowded with people drinking, shouting over the music, hustling one another, that there was nowhere for him to go. The drunk stayed upright, blinking, spilling the beer of the guy in the cowboy shirt in front of him.

Over on Amsterdam the well-dressed, polite young crowd at Sweetwater were waiting for the show to start — Thelma Houston — and listening to a Marvin Gaye song on the juke in the meantime.

On the streets the traffic was light, pedestrians few.

The wino on the center-strip divider of Broadway at 69th had quit tap dancing. Now he was sitting on a bench, waiting for the right woman to pass by, a suitable target for attack. His attack was always the same. *"When ya gonna wake up and smell the coffee?"* he'd growl. The words seem to yap inside him like hostile puppies. Without a woman around they could not get out. He needed to be free of them but without the appropriate woman he could not. He pulled on the dark brown bottle and watched and waited.

Inside MacDonald's Jim "Jumma" Jackson entered and looked around and sauntered to the counter. The girls behind the counter smiled at him. Jumma was a handsome man. He ordered three Big Macs and a chocolate shake, large order of fries.

He carried the plastic tray to his table and sat down, arranging his coat so that the gun lay flat in his raincoat pocket against his leg and would not dislodge itself accidentally. He was not at all nervous. The nervousness would come later, when he went back to the counter and pulled the gun. For now he just looked around.

An old woman sat muttering to herself a few tables back. Homeless, all her shit stuffed into shopping bags at her feet. He watched her pick at the ulcerous sores on her legs, scratch her dirty face.

No trouble there.

No trouble anywhere he could see.

A couple of Chinese kids on dates, eating cheap. An old guy.

A few tables down there was a brother with the twitchy kind of eyes that marked you for a booster, strictly small-time — hot watches, teeshirts, rings. That shit. He'd known some real good boosters in his day. One sister in particular who was so fucking good she could boost a full mink coat out of Bendel's or Bergdorf's, stuff it between her legs and walk right out of there.

None of it was trouble.

He nibbled his fries. He figured he'd wait till the booster drifted. You never knew. Could be somebody's boyfriend, one of the girls behind the counter, and you could never say when some motherfucker'd go all Bruce Lee on you.

You take your time, he thought.

He sipped the shake and ate his burgers, the weight of the pistol reassuring at his side.

At the kiosk at 72nd Street Mary Silver handed the man his change. If the man knew her and could have read her smile, he'd have seen the contempt there.

She sold the shit but she didn't have to like it,

Screw, Playboy, Penthouse, Jugs. They were all the same to her. Night after night she sat on the stool behind the newsstand surrounded by the stuff.

It was always a man who would buy. Never a woman. Not once.

And always the contempt was there. Another guy in rut without a place to put it.

A woman in tights and Nikes handed her two dollars for a copy of the Sunday *Times.* She made change.

"Thanks," she said. This time the smile was genuine.

On Saturday nights it was mostly the Sunday *Times* and the Sunday *News* people were buying, and that made Saturday nights okay in her book. By six o'clock the front sections were delivered and she and the boys would put them together by nine — and after that most of her business was papers, not porn.

She could remember a time when it hadn't mattered. She'd even been curious enough to look at the stuff.

That was before the fat man with the scars on his neck and the breath that stunk of Dentyne gum and cigarettes who — in the process of raping her, while his big hands were on her breasts and her own on his cock, trying to get his sad deflated cock up so he wouldn't turn lunatic and kill her — had said she looked like something out of *Playboy.*

Playboy.

Nice. It was supposed to be a compliment.

It was right after that that she'd decided to take the course in Dim Ching and Karate and started keeping the twelve-inch blade beneath the counter at night. And started hating pornography.

She'd discussed it with the women in her group. They all had reached the same conclusion. There was no excuse for porn other than to debase women. It was an instrument of terror, pure and simple — the patriarchal society keeping the girls in line by turning them into boy-toys. As far as she was concerned Guccione, Goldstein and the others were as bad as Hitler — freaks and genocides, all of them.

There was irony here.

The only reason she'd gotten into the business in the first place was that she'd looked around one day and realized that in all of Manhattan there wasn't a single newspaper kiosk run by a woman. She'd decided to change that. She'd . . . infiltrated.

She'd found that there were simply no profits in newspapers. It was all in cigarettes and magazines.

Skin-mags were the biggest draw of all.

So she had herself a situation here. She'd decided not to buy the kiosk.

"Thanks," she said as yet another asshole handed her a ten dollar bill for a copy of *Penthouse.* She gave him back his change.

Most nights she could carry this off with some measure of philosophy. She had an application in as manager over at Barnes & Noble — this was just temporary. But tonight she was having a hell of a time. Her head was throbbing. She'd been popping aspirin all evening but it didn't seem to help. If one more creep eyed her breasts beyond the wall of newspapers she just might murder the bastard.

It'll pass, she thought.

But it did not pass, as the night drew Mary Silver slowly down to morning.

"Five copies at $6.95," said Sheldon. "Three at $7.50."

Lydia ticked them off on her checksheet.

Sheldon took a step down on the ladder to begin the next row of books — they were on the hard-boiled section now in the back of the store — lost his footing, and damn near tumbled off the ladder.

"Sheldon! Watch it for god's sake!"

Sheldon just looked at her.

"Jeez, Lyd. I was the one who almost broke his neck here, you know?"

He was right. She was being testy. Inventory was almost finished.

Another hour or so and they could get out of here. She was exhausted, though. And nervous somehow. Keyed-up. She guessed that was the price you paid for a little extra enjoyment sometimes. She was supposed to have driven back to town early last night from her week in Davis Park but things with Ross had been so good she'd decided to stay the night and return this morning. Then they'd been sort of slow getting started — slow getting out of bed, actually — and there was that awful tie-up on Riverside Drive, and now they were running incredibly late.

Sheldon was good even to be there at this hour and here she was yelling at him.

"Sorry, Sheldon."

"It's all right."

It was the oddest thing, though. She could not get Ross out of her mind. The inventory was important — damned important when you were the owner and looking at another rent increase three months from now — but all she could think of was Ross.

She kept feeling him inside her. Actually feeling it.

She could close her eyes and see him naked and feel the strokes.

God! were it not for the inventory she could've stayed where she was and at this very moment they'd be . . .

She felt faint.

And she felt regret.

But she could not have left the job to Sheldon. Sheldon was sweet but he was working here because he loved books, not money. He could knew every book by John D. MacDonald and Elmore Leonard practically by heart but he could barely make change of a quarter. No head for figures at all. Left to him the inventory would have been a shambles.

As it was she'd had to watch him like a hawk. He'd miss whole clusters of books, skip them over completely despite the bottle-thick glasses he was wearing, and Lydia would have to point this out to him. He'd blush beneath the blister of pimples. Sorry.

He was sweet but exasperating. Especially after five hours on the road and five more here in the store.

And these . . . images that kept distracting her.

Time for a break, she thought. The last hour would probably go faster anyway if they had a little coffee in them.

"Come on down, Shel. Let's take five."

"Great." He climbed down off the ladder and wiped his dusty hands on his rumpled short-sleeve shirt.

Lydia took off her own glasses and put them on a pile of books beside her and rubbed her tired eyes.

Immediately the images returned. Ross inside her, his hands on her breasts. Her breasts actually tingled.

She blushed and turned away.

She poured them each some coffee and handed a cup to Sheldon and sat down.

Can he tell? she thought. Just by looking at me?

She felt that transparent.

He was eyeing her somewhat . . . appreciatively.

She was not what you'd call beautiful. Too short, for one thing, a bit too small on top and a bit too wide in the bottom, attractive but sort of plain-looking. She had spent a good portion of her life watching carefully for those appreciative looks — which rarely came. So she knew one when she saw it.

Could Sheldon have a crush on her?

She hoped not. For his sake.

Sheldon was just terminally gawky. And there was Ross.

She sipped the coffee.

Something stirred inside her, a memory that was only half a memory, Ross squirming sweating writhing deep inside her.

She heard the wall-clock ticking behind her. She felt faint again, held on to the wooden stool she was sitting on until it passed and stared at the wall of books.

And for Lydia too, the night wore on.

The Bar

MacInery's was nothing special but he liked it there. The place was small and dark, about a dozen seats at the bar and twenty tables crammed together toward the back, serviced by a small kitchen.

There was a red brick fireplace opposite the bar which they actually used in winter and which even now sported half a dozen logs piled on the grate and an antique stand for the shovel, poker and tongs. There were cut flowers on the mantle over the fireplace and hanging plants over the tables along with low-slung green-shaded lights which made each table look as though there were a poker game in progress.

It was a comfortable place, relaxed. Even on a night like this with the crowd three deep at the bar.

He ordered a second scotch from Bailey.

Bailey was a friend by now. He'd known him for years. Closed the place up with him plenty of times and helped him stack the chairs while they had a couple on the house with the lights low and door locked behind them. When Bailey was drunk he just slowed down.

You could wait five minutes for him to finish a single sentence while he stroked that blonde-red Berserker beard of his and sipped his beer and took his time thinking things through — but when the sentence did come out it was not going to be stupid.

Tom had never seen him lose control.

He could not exactly say that of himself.

He leaned back against the fireplace and watched the waitresses shuttle back and forth from the kitchen. Every table was filled and Chris, Erica and Rita were obviously having a pretty busy night of it. Erica looked particularly beat. As beat as a woman that good-looking was ever going to look. He watched her toss her long dark hair and slump exhausted at the bar at the waitress station, handing Bailey a check. You could almost read her mind. One more down and good riddance.

One of the cooks — Dom or Dominick, something like that — came trotting out of the kitchen and asked Bailey for a beer. Bailey poured him one, fast, and the man scuttled back toward the kitchen, wiping sweat off his face with his free hand.

He passed Erica serving drinks to a table of four, smiled and patted her once on the ass. She shot him a glance. The glance said it would be her great pleasure to skin him alive right then and there.

He guessed there was trouble again in the kitchen.

There was a woman he recognized standing by the jukebox. He'd seen her in here a number of times and wanted no part of her. She drank too much and turned ugly when she did. And she was already more than halfway in the bag. Something flickered across her face that was part scowl and part come-on as she ran her finger along the list of song-titles. Somebody would take her home tonight — but it wouldn't be him.

There was a very pretty woman at the telephone and two more — just kids, really — talking beside him. Another pair at the bar and a thin blonde in a red sweater who appeared to be drinking alone.

Alone if you didn't count the scruffy guy in khaki who was drunkenly, clumsily coming on to her. He watched her shake her head no and smile. Great profile. Lovely pale complexion. The guy hung on a while, then shrugged and turned away. He saw his opening and made for it.

Ladies' Night

She was drinking bloody marys.

Her arms were slim, the hands graceful.

He stood beside her, talking to Bailey, establishing that he was known here, safe to talk to, finishing his scotch and ordering another. Bailey knew the drill. The fact was that good bartender could do half your work for you. And Bailey was a good bartender.

She was listening. She couldn't help it. The guy beside her was listening too — Tom could see him sinking lower onto his stool in slow alky oblivion.

Then Bailey pulled his usual masterstroke.

"Tom? Do you know Cindy?"

An introduction. She smiled and turned and they shook hands. Her eyes were deep blue and wide and absolutely gorgeous.

He owed Bailey on this one. He'd say so.

Later.

Bailey poured a rum and coke and watched Tom Braun laughing talking to Cindy. Good to see somebody having fun, he thought.

The bar's a little weird tonight.

He'd thought that maybe you'd have to have worked here night after night to notice it so he'd mentioned it to Erica. But Erica just gave him a look. So he'd thought, well, maybe it's my imagination — but he didn't really believe that. Since he'd come on at six, before the bar was even very busy, he'd been aware of some kind of thickness in the air, a kind of tension, a sort of manic strain to the conversation. Like the night was coiling up for something.

He'd seen it before.

New Year's Eve was always pretty strange, and Saint Patty's Day, and sometimes even Christmas, when the bar was filled with people too lonely to have anywhere else to go. He remembered working a union bar once on a night after a long hard trucker's strike had ended — how the room was charged with a high mix of rising spirits and downright bloody murder. The kind of night when for whatever reason fights break out and drunks get dangerous and you kept your eyes open and an empty bottle handy just in case.

It was irrational, maybe, but he had one now behind the bar rail.

Because of the strangeness.

Since six o'clock he'd been feeling it, a sense of disquiet just below the surface. And despite Erica's response to him he thought that the waitresses must be feeling it too. They were all a little distant tonight, working their jobs like it was sheer drudgery — when usually they managed to have some fun here. It was that kind of place.

So actually he was glad to have been able to give Tom a hand with Cindy.

That, at least, was normal.

He wondered what Susan did the nights Tom was out prowling. Or how she took it in the morning. He liked Susan, even though he didn't know her as well as he knew Tom. Not for him to judge. But this kind of stuff was not terrific for a marriage.

Down at the end of the bar a woman was crowing for a gin and tonic. He poured it for her, thinking he was going to have to cut this one off soon if she kept on slugging them down like this, unusual for a woman to get so loaded so fast and so intently, thinking this carrying the drink over to her and looking at the two young girls who for some reason were standing there glaring at him over by the jukebox, when the weirdest fucking notion occurred.

What if it was the women?

Customers, waitresses.

What if it was all of them?

Nah, he thought. You're losing it. That's nuts.

But he looked around. He poured and served and looked around.

And the thought refused to go away. Every time there was the slightest lull in business the thought would prick at him and he'd feel the thickness start to rise in the room and the walls start to close a little.

It wasn't the guys.

It was the women who kept reminding him of those truckers blowing off steam after four months of no pay and no work and the wife and kids howling, who reminded him of bad Christmas Eves and bad Saint Patrick's Days.

It was the women.

And then he thought, that's bullshit, just look at Cindy sitting there with Tom, nice woman, everything fine. Check her out. Look at her looking at him like she'd like to reach over and just . . .

. . . eat him up.

I'm gonna have to watch this closely, he thought.

Troubled Sleep

The wind was hot.

It was a burning wind — it burned through Susan's sleep like acid on silk, reaching deep into each smooth furrow of her body. The nightgown was too much. Her breasts felt as though covered with sand, with insects, as though she lay buried to the neck in an anthill in a hot summer storm. By turns it was terrible and then sweet — a tickling, moving, crawling sensation. An awareness of the physical that not even sleep could override.

Her fingers moved to the neck of her nightgown, traveled down its front and parted it over her body. The feeling remained but it was better now, more purely pleasure, less frightening in the complexity of its overwhelming sensuousness.

Her tongue moved over dry cracked lips. Her fingertips went to her breasts, plucked the nipples up, caressed them as through layers of sand. A groan escaped her open mouth into the blasting wind.

What was that?

Elizabeth sat bolt upright in bed, listening.

Some sort of cry.

The sound had poured through her sleep, snatched her into wakefulness, its final tendrils dragging over her like scraps of vine.

It had come from outside.

She leaned toward the window, her fingernails brushing the wire-mesh screen. She looked down through the branches of the tree to the street. It was empty. A gust of wind slid a sheet of newspaper along the sidewalk, rustled the shrubbery below. The entrance to the building was silent.

A dream, she thought.

The newspaper lay stirless in the gutter. She listened to the sounds inside her apartment. The clock ticking, the distant hum of her refrigerator, the dense silence.

She was beginning to feel sleepy again.

Something screamed, it sounded like a child's scream and just beyond the screen something hurtled through her field of vision, a sudden pale blinding flash of movement.

Then stopped.

And meowed.

A cat.

A slim white cat with a black-spotted tail.

You little shit, she thought. You scared me half to death.

The cat stared in at her wide-eyed, wary. It paced the ledge. Must have come from the floor above, she thought. Living dangerously, making a jump like that.

Her heart was still pounding.

The cat sniffed the ledge and window-screen, its pink nose twitching. It gazed at the tree and seemed to contemplate the downward climb. Then it glanced back at Elizabeth. It did not seem terribly comfortable with her there, close enough to touch were it not for the screen. She wondered why. Cats usually took to her immediately.

Poor thing. It really did look scared out there.

The tip of its ear was missing.

There was only a little blood, it wasn't much more than a scratch, but the wound looked very recent. The blood was still glistening. Catfight, she thought. The eyes looked alert, frightened.

Ladies' Night

Frightened of her. She could swear it.

"What's the matter?" she whispered.

It was as though she'd hit it with a stick. The cat jumped out onto the nearest branch, ran to the main trunk of the tree and then raced suddenly down, disappearing into the shrubs below.

She watched until it was out of sight and then fell back away from the window into the cool softness of her bed. She lay a moment staring at the shadows playing across the ceiling and then closed her eyes.

Too bad, she thought. I could have patched her up a little.

The cat's amber-yellow eyes appeared before her, bright and full of some strange knowledge, before she fell asleep.

Barflies

This lady is terrific, he thought.

Close quarters had revealed a number of things. Slim waist, small firm breasts beneath the tight white sweater — with mercurial nipples that went hard or soft according to some runic chemistry, some internal winds of change — pale, smooth skin and delicate collarbones, a long and graceful neck, and full wide lips. Which smiled at him frequently.

Her name was Cynthia Jackson and she lived on 74th Street just off Central Park West. She was probably ten years younger than Tom and did not seem to mind the fact that he was older, she had a sister from Chicago whose visit last week she'd found very trying, and she was a photo-retoucher by trade and worked at home.

She in turn had elicited from him that he was an editor and that he was both married and had a child. This did not seem to faze her either.

If they got by Andy they were usually interested.

So that when she got up to use the john he knew she'd be back.

He ordered another round of drinks and watched her walk past the tables to the ladies' room, tight jeans promising equally fine slopes of leg and thigh.

It was only when the drinks arrived that he noticed the woman beside him.

She was drunk, leaning low over the bar. Not much to look at to start with and getting much worse by the moment. Scrawny inside a faded red teeshirt and tired-looking.

She smiled at him.

"Hi," she said.

She licked her lips.

Uh-oh, he thought. This one wants to talk.

"I'm gonna make you a promise," she said. Her words slurred together like a bad erasure.

"Shoot."

"Somebody don't give me a job soon, say one week, I'm gonna fucking murder myself. I swear it."

"Uh-huh."

"Waitress job. HMV. Anything. One week and then the hell with it, I'm checking out. That asking too much? Job as a waitress in a place like this?"

"No."

"Damn right. It's something to me, though." She took a slug of what appeared to be a gin and tonic.

"Look," she said. "I'm not stupid. Just finished my dissertation. Been writin' it three and a half weeks — first time out in nearly a *month.* So what do I do? Go out and drink up what's left of my money. In a joint like this. Drink so much I can hardly talk to anybody. Nobody to talk to in a month and now I can't talk to anybody. That make sense to you?"

"No. You're doing okay, though."

"Thank you. But doncha see it's self-destructive? I gotta have something *normal* happen to me. Got to make some money. Maybe waitress. 'S normal. People tip you. Know how much it *costs* to write a dissertation? How much they *charge* you for the privilege of writing yourself to death? Lotta money."

"What was the dissertation?"

"Schizophrenia."

He could think of nothing to say to that so they drank their drinks.

What a mess, he thought. Hair long, limp and tangled. Skin the color of mushrooms. Eyes all red and bleary — they were disturbing eyes. Beneath the weird conversation you could sense real pain, and a lot of it, just below the surface. Beneath the eyes there was something else. He didn't know what and didn't want to.

"It's the dissertation's made me crazy," she said, almost to herself. "Dissertations break up a lot of marriages, you know that? 'S very common." She waved her hand in dismissal. "Me, of course, I ain't married."

He saw Cindy walking toward him through the crowded tables.

"You'll be all right," he said.

"Sure I will. 'Course I will."

Bailey was looking at them and Tom nodded toward the woman. *Better cut her off,* the nod said. Bailey nodded back.

"Friend of yours?" said Cindy, sliding onto the barstool.

There was a cattiness there he didn't like. It surprised him. She hadn't seemed the type. It was as though between the time she'd left the bar and the time she returned something had changed about her.

"We just met," he said. His tone was cool.

"That's nice," she said, a sardonic smile playing at the corners of her mouth.

But he saw that his tone of voice had not been lost on her. She was staring directly into his eyes. And the look on her face said, *I'm taking you home tonight. So don't be a pain in the ass, please. Not over her, anyway. Relax and enjoy it.*

He looked at her. She was lovely. He guessed that compassion should have its limits.

The drunk was not long for the world anyhow. Her eyes kept closing. *The long blink,* his father used to call it. There was always a hotplate down at the end of the bar with a full pot of coffee going and Bailey was pouring her a cup.

He brought it over. Said something to get her attention.

She waved him away. Lurched suddenly to her feet and began to wobble through the crowd toward the door.

"Hey!"

Her purse was lying on the bar.

The woman stopped.

"Your purse," Tom said.

She wobbled back to them. Tom handed it to her and she smiled.
The smile was pretty ghastly.

"Thanks," she said. Then her smile faded. *"Thank you very much."*

She wasn't thanking him for the purse. She was thanking him for
talking. He felt a wave of pity. Even concern. There was something so
final about the way she'd thanked him — as though they were the last
words she ever expected to utter. He'd not given it much credence
before but maybe the woman was a potential suicide after all, maybe
she was serious and this last drunken lurch back through a crowd of
strangers for a pocketbook she did not much care about and would not
need where she was going was the end of it.

Jesus, he hoped not.

He watched the door close behind her. Through the window he
could see her ascend the stairs.

Maybe not, he thought. Drunks were full of drama.

He saw that Cindy was watching her too, very closely. Her eyes
were distant.

He heard a loud shriek of laughter from one of the tables behind
him. He turned.

In a corner to the back of the room a woman was standing — she
was one of a party of four — shaking with laughter. She had just
poured her drink down the shirt of the small balding man in tie and
jacket beside her, probably her date. The other tables had noticed and
the laughter was loud and general. Even Erica, their table's waitress,
stood there laughing.

The man stood up to shake the ice cubes off him, his bald head red
and gleaming.

He wasn't smiling.

The Boot's Last Purse

The Boot and Jimmy Diamond stood across the street two doors down in front of the barber shop and watched the woman leave McInery's.

They watched her weave past the cleaners, bobbing her head like a chicken, tits sliding every which way under the faded red teeshirt, purse dangling loosely from her hand. Boot had to laugh. She was exactly what they needed. A real stone alky they had here.

They waited till she got to the corner and disappeared down Riverside. Then they crossed the street and started after her.

The lady was barely conscious. Boot had his blade ready inside the jacket pocket but that was just a precaution. This was gonna be easy.

They picked up the pace. No sense her getting home before they reached her. You grab a purse, that was one thing. She opens her door, that's B&E, and there was no point upping the stakes for the same damn take. From the look of her she wouldn't be carrying much. But she'd been to a bar. And bars cost money.

It was dark on Riverside. Streetlights out in a couple of places, thank you New York City. They hung tight to the shadows and closed the distance. Boot had a look around. The street was empty. A new Mercedes glided by and passed them. He gave the nod.

They broke into a run.

Streetside, Boot went for the purse-strap while Jimmy Diamond came up directly behind her *and they had this down, man, really down, because the moment Boot touched the strap Jimmy would push her in the gutter, they had done it a hundred times by now, best team in the city.* And it happened just the way they played it. Boot hit the strap and Jimmy Diamond slapped her back hard with the palms of both hands and stepped away.

Only she didn't go down.

Drunks fell down. Women, you could push them.

But this one just stuck out her fucking leg to brace against the impact and at the same time whirled so fast he'd never have believed it in a million years, whirled on Jimmy Diamond and got hold of his arm.

And then she sort of *pulled herself onto him.*

Crawled onto him like some sort of bug — only fast, real fast, looking like maybe a spider would look to you if you were another bug and about to be eaten.

You could see Jimmy's face go grey, even though it was dark, even though it happened in just a second. She had him belly-to-belly with her legs wrapped around him like she was going to fuck the sonovabitch, like she *wanted* to fuck him, hips moving against him like that and it was grotesque, man, it was almost funny for a moment until the one hand came off his shoulders while the other tightened around his neck and Jimmy pulled back because he could see where that free hand was going but there was nothing he could do about it, the hand clawed across his eyes and Boot blinked his own eyes watching it, he could almost feel the pain himself and when the blink was over so were Jimmy's eyes.

There was blood pouring down his face. Boot screamed. They both screamed.

And the women let Jimmy go then and turned to Boot.

He'd never moved so fast in his fucking life. Because there was nothing in that face you recognized as human. Well, there was one thing, *it was smiling*. But it was not a smile you could look at without getting scared sick that such a thing existed. It was not just crazy. The face looked at him the way a sewer rat had looked at him once down by the East River, eyes red with the pure love of biting and killing.

And this face *smiled*.

He did not look back or worry about Jimmy. Four blocks away he got the guts to turn and saw she wasn't following. Another two blocks and he realized he still had her purse dangling from his fist.

He stopped and opened it half-blindly, breathing hard, not even knowing why he was doing it except it was the right thing to do, it was normal, you stole a purse you went through it.

He turned it inside out on the sidewalk.

Lipstick. Hairbrush. Matches from McInery's. Gum. Scraps of dirty paper. He found the wallet and opened it. There was a single dollar bill inside and a dime and a nickel in the change compartment.

It was the worst night of Boot's life.

And it was just beginning.

Strange About Mom

Andy didn't know what the noises were at first but they woke him from his dream.

He was at summer camp climbing a mountain. There were shade-trees all around. The quiver of arrows was slung over his back — though for some reason the bow was missing — and the scout knife was in his hand. The knife was open to the big blade because there was something on the mountain he was supposed to be afraid of. He wasn't really afraid, though. He felt sure that whatever was up there wouldn't hurt him. The knife was just in case.

As he climbed, though, the nature of whatever was up there began to change. He didn't know how he knew that but he did. At first it was a cat like a mountain lion, then something insect-like whirring out of sight above his head as he crawled up the rockface. Then he was walking past a storefront, somehow not out of place there, and knew that whatever it was, it was inside the store now and had changed again.

He was opening the storefront door when something woke him.

It sounded as though she was crying.

He pushed off the covers and got out of bed and peered into the hallway, listening.

She was crying all right. *In her sleep?*

For some reason he felt she was asleep.

Little liquid crying sounds. And the breathing wasn't right.

He wondered if he should go in there. If he was wrong and she was awake, she might feel bad about him seeing her like that. He didn't want to make her feel bad. He walked out into the hall.

She'd left the door open. There was light in the room from the streetlight. He could walk by, pretend he was going to the bathroom, take a peek and keep on going. That way if she *was* awake he wouldn't have to embarrass her. He rubbed the sleep from his eyes, assumed what he thought was a normal, going-to-take-a-whiz-in-the-middle-of-the-night pace, and walked by. And stopped.

She was alone. His father wasn't there.

She was asleep.

And she was naked.

He was not supposed to see her that way.

She was lying atop the covers with her nightgown open, naked underneath. He had never in memory seen his mother naked before.

He had never seen what she was doing either.

Not in real life. In some of the R-rated movies they rented sure and even then you didn't see much. But not a real woman.

Not his mom.

He felt dizzy. A wave of heat passed over him, then a wave of chilling cold.

There was something . . . *not right* about it.

It wasn't the masturbation. He knew about masturbation — at least he knew people did it, though he'd never heard of anybody doing it in their sleep before. And it wasn't just that it was his mother either. Though it was partly that.

It was the *sounds*.

Whimpering, crying.

Then growling. Low in her throat like an animal.

He didn't know how he dared but he moved closer, into the room, a few feet from the bed.

She was sweating. Her body was coated with sweat, plastering back her hair, pooling where her breasts pressed together trembling — trembling because both hands were down there now, her legs spread wide and the fine pale hair of her thighs dewy with sweat and one of her hands — *God! her* whole *hand!* — glistening with what was inside her. She was writhing like a snake. He saw four fingers disappear inside her to the knuckle and the other hand rubbing something wet outside and there was that noise, that hissing, crying, groaning sound like she was in pain, like she was dying!

Run! he thought.

No! *Wake her!*

But he was afraid to wake her and it was as though he were hypnotized, he *couldn't* run. He was afraid to wake her because he stared down at what her hands were doing and the teeth grinding and the lips quivering as though from some biting cold and the awful trembly smile and he didn't even hardly recognize her, he was *scared* of her, *what had happened to his mother?*

His stomach rolled and tumbled. He was going to be sick.

He watched the hand glide back and forth, the head toss and shudder.

He ran. He stumbled into his room. The dizziness was terrible. He fell into bed, trembling, sweating now almost as much as she had been. He pulled the covers up to his chin — the first time since the second grade. He really *did* have to go to the bathroom now but he was not going to pass that door again. No way.

He listened. The sounds had stopped.

Had she heard him? Was she awake, coming toward the bedroom?

He heard nothing.

Maybe she's asleep now, he thought. Really asleep.

Outside his window he heard a siren, a police car rolling by. His hands on the bedsheet looked ghostly pale. The room seemed filled with shadows.

He lay there for a long time, listening and hearing nothing, remembering the look of her, the dark full nipples against the pale breasts, the glistening public hair, the streams of sweat. He remembered her face most of all, that rictus grin of pain and ecstasy. Remembered it with horror.

Horror, he thought. And I thought it was monsters and Freddy Kruger.

Slowly, a long time later, he was able to push the vision away from him. In the long silence his eyes began to close. The shadows folded back into the ordinary landscape of the room — dresser, closet, tv set, window.

Once he seemed to hear her sigh.

She sounded as she always sounded.

Night and the City

There might have been an inkling on the evening news. It might have saved lives if there had been. But as yet little anyone would consider particularly newsworthy had happened. What slept inside them slept like a malefic shadow in the corner of a huge bustling room, unnoticed.

By the time it erupted, for many residents of Manhattan the night had concluded normally. They had made love, gone to films and bars, watched television. And finally, slept.

If there appeared to be somewhat more police activity than usual on the lower West Side or Chelsea or Central Park South, it was just another busy night for the city's numerous thugs and crazies. If a disturbance erupted in a theatre it was hardly the first time.

Only on the West Side could you tell immediately — something so askew now that stepping out of the subway at 72nd Street your impulse might be to turn and run. Elsewhere it was simple city madness, more virulent than usual. But here, in the very feel of the place, you sensed something.

On Amsterdam and 66th Street a woman walked into a fire station wearing nothing but a black half-slip and, laughing, accosted the nearest fireman, smearing his face with cruelty-free Flame-Glo Honey Raisin Lip Gloss, which she had applied on her own face from nose to chin.

Across the park on 5th and 81st Street, an old man recuperating from his second coronary in as many years leaned out his fifth-floor window and heard someone crying for help just out of sight around the corner. The voice was male and terrified. Heart pounding, he closed the window.

On the northernmost border of Greenwich Village, a normally quiet lesbian bar called Belle Starr's erupted into an orgy the likes of which its proprietor, an ex-stripper named Lorna Dune, hadn't seen since Albert Anastasia was alive and she was still more or less straight.

In Soho, an aging ingenue hung her two-month-old infant son from the bathroom shower-curtain rod using the white cloth belt she had worn as the Girl in *The Fantastiks* and watched it strangle.

At 42nd and Broadway, three dancers in a peep show hurled themselves through the nearest fifty-cent window and dragged its occupant screaming through the broken glass.

The drunk at Broadway and 69th woke on his bench to stare at the world through sore, soupy eyes. Someone had kicked his bottle.

He was keyed to that sound. It was probably the only sound that would have woke him. He reached for the bottle instinctively beneath the flaking weatherbeaten green park bench but the effort was far too much for him. He wheezed a sigh and leaned back against the bench.

"Let me help you."

The voice was young and female. He looked up. The woman stooped beside him fishing for the bottle. Her hair was short, cropped close to her head. He didn't much care for that. He liked a woman to be feminine.

"When ya gonna wake up and smell the coffee?" he rasped.

Ladies' Night

The woman raised her head and stared at him. Not bad looking despite the hair. She picked up the half-empty fifth.

"Hey, ya found it. Good girl!"

She smiled. "It's broken, though," she said.

"Izzit?"

He tried to focus.

The girl was nuts. The bottle wasn't broken.

"Is not," he said.

"Sure it is," she said, and swung it in a short arc, smashing it against his mouth and chin. His last two brittle teeth shattered into his chalky gums. He tasted blood and shards of glass redolent of sweet wine. He tried to spit them out but his lips were in tatters.

Nothing hurt, though. Nothing ever hurt till morning. If he had another fifth maybe not even then. So fuck her.

He'd survive.

He made a face, the kind of face he used on the little girls to scare them of the drunk, to scare them home to their fucking mommies.

The girl was looking at him like he was some sort of bug.

She was the bug.

"Why doncha wake up . . ." he tried to say but the words only gurgled in his mouth and pushed a long shard of glass he wasn't even aware of out over his chin. He coughed, and that was bloody too.

And the girl wasn't scaring.

He didn't like her eyes.

He thought, this is gonna be bad — and then it *was* bad, because the hand with the pretty gold ring drew back the bottle and then pushed it forward into his face and twisted it so that it tore a jagged trench of flesh from the bridge of his nose across both cheeks and down as far as his lower lip.

She released it and the bottle stayed there, like a false-face made of glass.

He felt a quick burning flash of unexpected agony and then passed out in broken shock, vomiting into the still-capped neck of the bottle. He gasped and began to choke. His face went livid blue.

At the newspaper stand on 72nd Mary Silver walked quietly away from the stack of papers and magazines which had surrounded her and, knife in hand, proceeded down Broadway.

The knife got a lot of use.

The first was a Greek who had just come out of the subway station after a strange little ride on the #2 line. A woman on his car, a black woman, had begun laughing at 14th Street and hadn't stopped until they reached Penn Station. Whereupon she leapt suddenly from her seat and began to kick the subway doors with her imitation patent-leather shoes. The other riders on the train had witnessed her fury with varying degrees of amusement. All except the Greek. The idiot sister he'd left on Corfu made any such amusement impossible. He left the subway blindly, lost in remembrance.

When Mary came up behind him he was still brooding on his sister and because the knife was sharp and the blade thin he felt no pain at first. His only thought was that the woman had punched him hard between the shoulderblades. Why she should do that he didn't know any more than he knew what had happened to the woman on the subway.

He felt the wetness seeping through his shirt and a sudden faintness overcame him and he fell to his knees. He died in that position, watching the woman continue past him down the street.

The second man was a young yuppie broker in suspenders and a baggy white Ralph Lauren shirt which set his Hamptons tan off nicely. As she passed him she stabbed him in the kidneys. The man watched the red stain spread over his shirt like burning celluloid on a movie screen. The shirt had been brand new. It cost him two hundred dollars.

At 70th Street she passed a fat old man and smiling, stabbed him in the ass. A playful gesture. The knife sunk only to the depth of an inch or so but the old man howled and tripped and fell to the pavement and lay sprawled there waving his hands and screaming.

She proceeded down Broadway, steel blade dripping.

He was staring at a copy of Jim Thompson's *The Killer Inside Me,* wondering if he should steal it. Lydia was still in the storage room and his jacket had big pockets. The cover of the book was badly ripped but his copy at home was falling apart completely. It would be like taking day-old bread from a bakery. Why not?

Ladies' Night

Because you're honest, that's why not, he thought. And because you like her.

Face it, you *more than* like her.

"Shel, come here a minute," she said.

He sighed and climbed off the ladder. He could guess what was coming. Lydia was going to ball him out again for something he'd done or failed to do — which would make it about the fifth time that night. She was in a pissy mood. Couldn't she see he was exhausted? Up the ladder, down the ladder.

Couldn't she see he was crazy about her?

Sure, she had ten years on him. She had a boyfriend and a business too but none of that mattered. He knew she loved books. They had that very much in common. They could talk books the next thirty years of their lives together given the opportunity. He knew it. He'd like to do just that.

That and . . . the other thing.

His shirt was plastered to his back. The air-conditioner wasn't working again. It was miserably close in here, so that his thick heavy glasses kept slipping down his nose. He pushed them back and walked to the storage room.

It was pretty dark. There was just the single 30-watt bulb she refused to change for a bigger one — Lydia was actually a little cheap, always saving on the electricity — and they could have used a new air-conditioner too. The light didn't do much more than push back the murk into the corners.

"Where are you?" he said.

"Back here."

He was relieved. She didn't sound mad at all.

He walked inside. The back room was wall-to-wall boxes set on rows of metal shelving, filled with books. They were the first things they'd inventoried.

So what was she doing back here?

The dust got into his nose and made him want to sneeze. He held his breath so he wouldn't have to. Even if he did love books he didn't much care for the old musty smell of them, like the smell of mold in a cellar. He thought he was probably a little allergic.

He heard shuffling to his right. *Over there.*

He stepped in front of the next row of shelves and saw her way down the end of the row, facing the grey cinderblock walls, her back to him, half in shadow, her head tilted down like she was reading.

In the dark?

"What's up, Lyd?"

She turned.

It wasn't reading.

What she'd been doing was she'd been working at the bottons of her shirt.

She was almost finished.

He couldn't believe it. All he could do was stand there gawking like a dope while she slipped the shirt off her shoulders and he saw that she had no bra on, that her breasts were naked — *and god she was pretty there!*

He braced himself against the metal shelving.

"Well? What do you think?" she said.

"Huh?"

She flipped open the top button of her jeans and zipped the zipper and pulled them down over her thighs, the thighs a little too big but that was okay because her stomach was nice and flat and she had lovely breasts and it was all so good he could barely look at her. But he did look. She smiled.

"What do you think?"

This wasn't like Lydia at all.

Lydia was his boss.

Lydia was . . . *modest.*

He couldn't believe his luck.

But he couldn't answer her, either. Not while he was looking at her body anyway. So he wrenched his eyes up to her face and held them there, determined, her face in shadow, looking at it anyway because it was the right thing to do even as she bent slightly to pull down the pale-colored panties and then stood a moment and then took one step toward him.

Out of the shadows.

And Sheldon wanted to scream.

Because the lips that were smiling at him were split in a dozen places and gleaming with blood, *her blood* where she had bitten them, bitten almost *through* them in some places and he started to say, Lydia, jesus ! what've you done? but he didn't really think there was a Lydia there anymore to talk to.

Her teeth were grinding so hard he could actually hear them. Her pale blue eyes looked contaminated with red, twitching in their sockets like caged birds. And he did not even consider seizure, epilepsy or something, because the look on her face was evil, terrible, the fear of her went right to his bones and he screamed, long and loud and yet without the strength to pull away as her cold arms wrapped around his neck and she opened her ruined mouth and bit him, deep into his neck and pushed him to the floor.

His glasses cracked beneath him. He heard his own blood pulse and splash the dirty concrete floor.

As consciousness raced away from him and she clung and bit deeper and he felt her tongue move inside the open wound he gazed up at the boxes above him and saw the one marked with red grease-pencil near his head and even upside down he could read it.

FILE UNDER HORROR it said.

On 73rd and Broadway in front of the Beacon Theatre a stewardess who had worked the first-class compartment on the very same flight that had brought Elizabeth in from LAX to Kennedy was walking her dog, a miniature poodle named Marvin, her pooper-scooper, toweling, and plastic baggie in hand, when a pair of teenage girls with leopard jackets and red and green hair jumped out of a '74 Chevrolet and approached the dog murmuring nice doggie, nice doggie, bent down and with one girl holding and the other pulling tore its head from its body.

Jim "Jumma" Jackson moved slowly off the yellow plastic seat and tossed his food wrappers and the cup from his shake into the trashbin.

It was about fuckin' time.

Over an hour, watching and waiting for the booster who was the only potential trouble in the place to get the hell out of there like he was doing now, ambling out the door.

He pretended to study the overhead menu, like here was a dude with one real big appetite back for seconds and then moved up to the counter.

It was only then he realized that there was nobody there.

What the fuck's this?

Break-time, bitches?

The Man went by outside, siren wailing. About the sixth in the past hour. But the squad car wasn't stopping here and that was what counted. He tapped the call-bell for some service.

Nobody home. *Come on,* he thought.

He couldn't even see the cook at work behind the rows of stacked-up burgers, fries and Big Macs. He tapped the bell again. He could hear the burgers working on the grill and he could smell the fat. He fingered the pistol in his jacket pocket.

"Hey! How 'bout gimme some service here!"

He glanced around the restaurant. The only one looking at him was the old bag-lady by the window. The kid and his girlfriend were playing at some touch-me shit. The old man wolfed his burger.

He hit the bell a third time.

"Hey! What the fuck you doin' back there!"

Easy; brother, he thought. *You be cool now.*

The bag-lady was grinning at him. The old man blinked up from his burger. The bag-lady wouldn't remember him, she was too fucking crazy but the old man might.

Got to be cool.

He saw movement behind the counter and the familiar uniform *finally!* One of the bitches was on her way out here.

But it was getting complicated now. The fucking old baglady was out of her seat and moving in his direction. No good. You didn't want nobody *near* you when you pulled this shit. Only way to handle it was to pull his piece right now and say fuck it.

Which was what he did.

The timing would be okay. He glanced at the girl coming toward him behind the racks of burgers. He slid the gun out of his pocket and turned and pointed it at the bag-lady.

"Hold it, bitch!" he said and she did.

Okay.

He turned to the girl who had come up beside him at the counter, turned cool and calm and pointed the gun at her face.

The girl was grinning.

And her face was covered with . . . what the fuck . . .?

. . . *catsup.*

Unh-unh. That shit was *blood!*

The girl's arms were long, a warm light-colored brown. They reached out to him. The palms of her hands were dripping. Blood spotted the counter.

He felt something knot up big as a man's fist inside his gut. Not fear — he had a gun on the girl for fuck's sake — but a shock of recognition, that old Jumma had maybe got outclassed by this one, that this bitch was bold as he was and a whole lot crazier, and all of a sudden he was wondering where the other bitches were and where the cook was and what the fuck was happening here.

He was wondering that when the bag-lady wrapped her arms around him and hugged him to her reeking body from behind and the gun went off in the counter-bitch's face so that she went down like a tree. He struggled but the bag-lady bitch only woofed in his ear and hugged him tighter.

Damn! she was strong. He couldn't break her.

He couldn't turn around!

He saw two more girls coming out from in back, drifting toward him like a pair of goddamn crazy ghosts and he fired at them but with only his forearm free of the bag-bitch the shots went wild. He didn't know how many times he fired but all of a sudden the gun was empty.

He squirmed and began to whimper, feeling righteous terror as the girls climbed up over the counter.

Behind him the front door slammed. Somebody on the run.

The girls reached out to him, their little brown uniforms and little brown caps splotched with blood — hands and faces too — and one of them had been *reaching into something* because her arms were wet and red to the elbow and *that was not no fucking hamburger.*

He smelled fat burning and the urinal stink of the woman behind him.

He began screaming when they opened the counter and hauled him back where the grill was, and then he was screaming so fucking loud one of them held his jaw open while the other reached inside and her polished red fingernails dug down and tore forward and he was looking at his tongue in her hand, he had stopped screaming and was spitting blood.

The pistol dropped from his hand.

When the faintness passed he looked up from the floor and saw the mess on the grill and knew what had happened to the cook. He felt the heat of the grill as they lifted him up and pressed his face slowly down.

Bitches, I was only gonna rob you! he thought. For that you gonna *fry* me?

The grill and Jumma sizzled.

Headcounts

Bailey was sure now. He'd never seen a bar like this. Not New Year's, not Christmas. *Never.* He felt a black flash of vertigo.

The bar spoke only in murmurs, in subtle waves of heat. Even the juke was silent. In some ways that was worst of all. It occurred to him that he'd been waiting for somebody to get up and feed it a quarter for fifteen minutes now.

Whatever was happening here he was part of it — *the nervous part.*

MacInery's had gone from crowded to damn near deserted in record time — and it was early yet, but nobody was coming *in.* He'd watched single guys and couples walk out the door, glancing around in what looked to Bailey like some weird sort of superstitious dread. And when his regulars left him — Sam and Bob and Tony — without so much as a word to him all doubts disappeared. Something was seriously wrong here, something fundamental.

Because other couples had left in a different way altogether.

Women leading their men like dogs on a leash — boyfriends, husbands, pickups — leading them as though into some impossible ravenous night, to something infinitely more private than anything they were expecting.

How did he know this?

He just did. They wore it on their faces.

He wiped the bar, served the drinks.

The place was charged with gunpowder. He was not about to go lighting any matches.

He poured a cup of coffee from the pot on the burner. There was not a soul in the bar whose exact location he wasn't aware of. He'd never watched so hard in his goddamn life.

That writer — Patty something — kept looking at him. He'd always liked Patty but not now. He dropped his eyes away from her and went back to work. A Ross Macdonald line scuttled through his mind unbidden, he remembered it because it had always reminded him of his former girlfriend. *The small chill presence that lived like a stunted child in her fine body.*

That was Patty now. Again he marked her position. *Seated, number two table, nursing a tequila sunrise.*

There were half a dozen women left at the tables, three at the bar.

Five men at the tables.

And only Tom, with Cindy, at the bar.

You had the two cooks, Dom and Franco, in the kitchen, and the three waitresses.

That was another thing. The waitresses *never* hung out in the kitchen. Too hot back there. Usually they liked to drink cokes out here with him and joke with the regulars. But not tonight. For the past half hour he'd hardly seen them.

He'd never felt so alone in a bar in his life.

The only regular that was left was Tom and he was, shall we say, *busy.* Cindy was keeping him busy. Like some of the others he seemed practically transfixed. Spellbound. The same glassy look half the other guys had tonight.

Nobody else seemed to worry about it. Just Bailey.

But the place was raw with sex.

Ladies' Night

Every guy in the place must have thought he was scoring.

In the farthest table to the right a couple were openly necking. It didn't seem to bother the guy at all that half an hour ago his date had dumped her drink all over his shirt. A little more and he'd have good cause to eighty-six the both of them. If he dared.

Which he didn't.

And right here at table four next to Patty a woman in jeans and halter top had her arm around the guy beside her and was fondling his nipple inside his Hawaiian shirt.

Jesus! Didn't they know this shit was *impossible?* Didn't these guys *feel* it?

Something was going down and sex was just part of it — and maybe only a small part of it. There was something else happening that was cold, androgynous, sexless. End-stop. Like death.

What he really wanted to do was to clear the goddamn bar.

He'd considered it a dozen times but it was nowhere near closing time and there was nothing to pin it to, no incident, and he was seriously afraid of starting one. But if nobody else sensed violence in the air, he did.

Take it easy, he thought and let things take their course. With a little luck and some patience you'll get out of here fine.

The woman in the halter top got up and reached for her date's hand. The guy in the Hawaiian shirt stood up beside her stuporous and smiling. She put her arm around him and they drifted out the door.

That left eleven.

And eight men.

He couldn't stop tallying, figuring the odds.

He glanced at the two women at the bar two seats down from Tom and Cindy. He got the same feeling from these two that you got from a bad drunk — only they weren't drunk. They weren't doing much of anything, not even talking. Just sitting there. But he could hardly look at them.

And one was downright beautiful. A tall willowy brunette.

The other was shorter, blond, kind of dumpy. But what they had in common was the eyes. He'd put their drinks down in front of them but he couldn't meet their eyes. Same with Patty.

Same with all of them.

These two were watching him, though. He knew it the way you knew somebody was staring at the back of your neck — you knew without knowing. Sending out strange little waves of allure. *Come talk to us. Come on.*

He wasn't having any.

His coffee tasted dark and sour. He dumped it in the sink. To hell with it. He'd made up his mind.

He was going to close the place.

Family emergency, he thought. It was stupid to wait. He was not going to be happy until he was back in his apartment with the door shut.

He was definitely closing.

He'd been trying to think what she reminded him of and Tom had it now. And he'd have left her right then and there had he not turned a corner with her long ago, had he not felt suddenly and without warning that blast of sensuousness that swirled out of her deep and greedy, a pure bold *vice* that made the sensuality of his wife and Elizabeth and every other woman he'd ever known seem childish by comparison.

She took his hand, pressed it between her own hands so he could feel the heat of her, brought it close to her face so he could feel her breath on his fingertips — and that was when he saw it, in the position of head and hands and knew what she reminded him of.

A mantis.

He'd watched them often as a child. Slow and deliberate until the final blinding moment of predation, alert and thoroughly voracious. A cannibal who would eat her mate and preferred to devour him alive. A death machine, quick and deadly, its huge mandibles unstoppable, forelegs gripping, the relationship of legs to head a sudden nexus of horror.

He had watched them eat.

This was what he recognized.

And didn't care.

Not while the urgent scent and electric closeness of her body continued to press him deeper into the wind and promise a burst of dreams.

Outside the bar, sirens and a sudden scream.
A man's howl of agony.

Bailey looked up from the register, wiped the sweat off his nose and stared hard through the windows.

The bar fell silent.

A man in a rumpled business suit ran by. The man looked over his shoulder and stumbled and then got to his hands and knees. Bailey heard the sound of a garbage can being knocked over as he disappeared from view.

It's starting, thought Bailey. It's right outside the window.

The silence in the bar seemed to hang from a single thread. A gust of summer wind whistled past the door.

And snapped it.

Tom thought, *what's funny?* What is that?

The laughter was Erica's, high and hysterical. She was moving through the kitchen doorway, a covered silver platter on a silver serving tray balanced precariously on her hand and shoulder and shaking with laughter so that he thought, she's going to drop that thing, Chris and Rita appearing behind her, laughing too as Erica's knees began to buckle.

He got up to help her and glanced at Bailey. The look on Bailey's face stopped him cold, made him hesitate.

The small balding man in the party of four wasn't as lucky. Tom could see the brown liquor-stain on his shirt as he reached out to take the tray and steady her. A good-looking young woman with long blonde hair stood up beside him. He had time to wonder, his *date?*

Then everything happened fast.

Erica stopped laughing — and the man no sooner had his hand on her shoulder than her own went to the cover of the serving tray and threw it off.

The man recoiled as though bitten by a snake.

From where Tom stood he had a clear view of them, his senses recording the scene in minute detail while his brain tried to do the impossible and process it *Dom, the cook, Mexican, illegally employed, thirty-six or so, flirts with the waitresses, awkward, miserable grasp of the language* and . . .

They'd hit him with something first, blood was dark and matted over his face and hair and lay in a ripe blackening pool at the bottom of the tray. His mouth and eyes were open. Protruding from the mouth was what at first looked like a tongue engorged in size and split into long attenuated segments that curled down at the ends into the bright gore pooling from the stump of neck — but it wasn't a tongue, it was a hand severed at the wrist and shoved deep down his throat, just the fingers and knuckles visible crawling from the mouth like a great pale spider flecked with blood.

He remembered how Dom had patted her earlier.

The kitchen door flew open and Chris and Rita moved to her side, the bald man stepping back and stumbling, terrified of the three of them and the thing on the plate, into the arms of the blonde at his table, her hand going to his chin and pulling his head back while the other hand went to his neck with the butter knife, and there were shouts and — horribly — *laughter* as the entire bar was suddenly on its feet, moving in a strange distorted adrenal rhythm and he felt a silent warning behind him.

Cindy.

He whirled and saw the two women at the bar reach for Bailey — but Bailey was ahead of them. His hand was already on the coffeepot. The coffee splashed scalding hot across the pretty woman's face and the pot continued on its arc across the face and head of the woman beside her, shattering.

Cindy was by the fireplace.

He knew instantly why.

He felt sudden panic and looked for a weapon.

She turned, poker in one hand and tongs in the other. Foam drooled and bubbled on her lips. He picked up a stool. Hurled it at her. It glanced off her shoulder and crashed into the clock behind her. She came on fast, snarling.

He vaulted the bar. The poker cracked down across the bar just above his head, splintering the wood.

Bailey was beside him just inches away. The woman on top of him was the one he'd hit with the coffeepot and there was blood flowing from the side of her face but it was not enough to stop her. His hands were on her shoulders trying to force her back but the woman's strength was amazing. Her legs were wrapped around him, squeezing, she was gaining on him by inches, crawling over him like an insect, mouth seeking his neck and fingers gripping him like fierce talons.

He got to his knees. He straight-armed the woman as hard as he could, the open palm of his hand slapping so hard against her forehead it jarred him to the shoulder, breaking her neck — so that her eyes rolled up white and a bubble of blood burst across her lips and Bailey shoved her off him like something contaminated, like a sac of poison.

The poker grazed his forehead and slammed into the shelf where Bailey kept the wineglasses, showering him with broken glass. Tom fell over on his back and somewhere behind him back in the restaurant heard more glass breaking like an echo and a long deep agonized cry. He looked up and saw the room painted in crazy swinging shadows, a dozen overhead lamps lurching and whirling all at once. He saw Cindy leaning over the bar like some sort of gargoyle leering down at him, the tongs in her left hand raised for another try.

He got to his knees and tried to move back but the tongs came down across his shoulder. He felt a sick dizzy pain rocket through his body. He started to fall again and put out his hand.

He felt a second bright slash of agony as a long sliver of glass slid seamlessly into the palm of his hand.

He howled and pulled the hand away. Pain wrenched at his stomach. He raised the hand and got to his knees again, fully expecting the next blow to fall and end him but he couldn't bear the glass there and the blow never came and fingers trembling he gripped and pulled away the gleaming shard and dropped it and pressed his hand to his thigh to stop the pulsing ooze of blood.

Bailey had come up fast behind the bar, a fifth of Dewar's in each hand.

The grinding helplessness he'd felt beneath the woman had turned to anger and even excitement now that open warfare had erupted all around him. He had Tom Braun to thank for saving his ass. He owed him one and that meant keeping the woman with the tongs and poker, the Cindy-thing, at bay. He'd seen Tom go down and the Cindy-thing come after him and he hefted the bottles.

She looked at him and stepped back, wary, her eyes full of fathomless calculation, a hunting animal faced with one of its kind. She took a small step back toward the jukebox and he pitched a bottle at her, a full unopened litre. Her reactions were good. She stepped away and brought the poker down and smashed the bottle, filling the air at once with the heavy reek of whiskey — but the move had skewed her balance and he heaved the second bottle and she couldn't move away.

It hit her in the neck and sent her sprawling back against the juke and Bailey thought *I've got you.* He grabbed a bottle of cognac and scrambled across the bar. On the jukebox Elvis started singing *Blue Hawaii.* He broke the cognac bottle across her face and that was that.

He had a moment to look around. The bar was careening its way to hell and the only thing left was to get out of there. There was a man lying face up across one of the front tables, the television set with its tube broken lying across his chest where they'd left it after using it to smash his skull. Another sprawled across the floor with a carving knife from the kitchen embedded in his back and Rita was just moving off the body.

The little bald man's drinking buddy was probably worst of all. They had him dangling from a coat-hook mounted on the wall, the hooks embedded in his back, arms and feet still twitching, blood sliding down off his chin. Erica stood gazing up at him admiringly.

There were only three of them now. Three men left in the bar Tom and him and some poor bastard huddled against the far wall with six of them converging on him like dogs on a dying bull.

He was a big man but they had him whining. You could see on his cheeks where they'd been at him with their nails or a fork or something, long straight scratches that looked deep. He was holding a chair in front of him like a lion-tamer in a circus but it was just a matter of time. Patty was leading them, leaning forward, squeezing her bared breasts in some passionate hallucinatory mockery and hissing like a snake. Behind her Chris was slashing the air with a butcher knife. The others crouched together like a grim silent slavering pack awaiting the kill.

The stench of insanity climbed high above the whiskey and fouled the air like heavy musk.

It was bad to leave him that way but there were too many.

He bent low and moved to the open panel under the waitress' station. Tom was still on his knees gripping his bleeding hand like that was the only thing in the goddamn room that mattered.

Shock, thought Bailey.

"Tom," he said. *"Braun."*

Bailey watched the glassy blankness in his eyes slowly vivify into recognition.

"Stay low. We've got to get out of here. Come on."

Bailey moved him through the panel and out in front along the row of barstools. Behind him the man was screaming. The sound vibrated through his bones. A wail of the stockyards, the screams of dying cattle. Tom froze ahead of him.

"Move, dammit!"

He wondered where the bottle in his hand had come from.

"Take it slow. Nice and easy. When we get outside head for Broadway. I'll be right behind you."

The screams stopped suddenly.

He heard footsteps pounding toward them and tables and chairs pushed over and thrown aside and he pushed Tom hard ahead of him.

"Go!"

He turned and Patty was coming at him with a broken whiskey glass, hands and face and breasts covered with blood, bloody handprints on her breasts, and the others were right behind her. Knives threw shivers of light across the ceiling. Lurid faces, incomprehensible.

He swung the bottle at her head and heard it smash and saw her fall away stumbling over Cindy's body beside the jukebox, back into the rest of them crowded into the narrow barspace. He had the fraction of a second he needed and he stooped and retrieved the tongs from under Cindy and turned and kicked the poker back to Tom at the door and heard him scoop it up.

Then they seemed everywhere at once.

He came up swinging and felt the tongs connect. Rita tumbled away from him clutching her forehead. He shoved the woman beside her and brought the tongs down behind her ear. The woman grunted and fell like a sack. Tom's poker nearly clipped his shoulder as it cracked down on Erica's wrist. Her knife clattered to the floor and Bailey chopped at her with the tongs, shattering her nose.

He had the tongs up again when Chris pushed the carving knife into his shoulder.

He heard the scrape of blade against bone. It seemed to vibrate through his body. For a moment he was blind in its awful clarity and felt himself start to fall. Thick acid filled his throat. He felt hands on his face, reaching for his eyes, his hair and he smelled the spice of much too much perfume and then two hands grabbed him from behind and flung him through the doorway.

He crawled through the cool breeze on scraped bloody knees, heard a door slam shut and the sound of metal on metal. He was on the sidewalk. He gave in to the feeling inside and vomited. He felt Tom's hand on his shoulder and then he was lifting Bailey to his feet. He heard glass breaking as Tom pulled the tongs from his hand — *he'd been clutching them all the time* — glanced back and saw that Tom had shoved the poker through the door's double handles and was beating at Chris with the tongs as she tried to crawl out through the window, slashing with the knife, her mouth drooling long white trails of spittle.

He felt a wave of anger and disgust and stepped toward her. Her knife darted out at him. He avoided it easily. He took one more step and kicked her in the chin as though she were a football, snapping her up through the jagged glass above and tumbling her back down into the bar.

He looked at Tom.

"Two points," he said. "Jesus."

"Can you run?" Tom was looking at his shoulder.

He heard them screeching inside, pounding at the door. Saw another appear at the window.

"I'll have to. Where?"

And suddenly it dawned on him. He knew what Tom would say before he said it. It froze and sickened him.

"Andy," he said. "My apartment. Andy's there."

Bailey did what he guessed Tom couldn't do and completed the thought.

Andy's there.

With Susan.

The Call-Up

When the call came through Lederer was in his Brooklyn apartment, lying on his bed. Straddled by his wife Millie.

"Aw, for chrissake," she said.

He reached for the phone and Horgan started talking and Millie stayed put for a while, but then he could feel himself recede inside her like some time-lapse movie of a water-starved plant and she got off him and lit a smoke.

He listened to Horgan, wondering if the guy had gone completely batshit loony on him since he'd left the precinct and then hung up the phone.

"That was the damnedest call I ever heard."

If it was possible for somebody to smile disgustedly then that was what she did.

"What," she said.

"We've got a citywide mobilization on your hands. Horgan's jabbering about the National Guard. He was his usual articulate self so it's hard to say what the hell's going on. And I was only halfway with him anyway."

Her smile brightened.

"I bet it's that goddamn tanker," he said.

"What tanker?"

"I told you. Over on Riverside. The one with no route sheet and the phony plates. But get this. They've got Lieutenant Anderson and Sergeant Dickenson in the cooler down there."

"Why?"

"That's what I said. Why? So Horgan says, 'they're women, aren't they?' Now what the hell do you make of that?"

He zipped his pants, found his shirt on the chair and put it on. He leaned over and kissed her cheek.

"That was nice," he said.

"While it lasted."

"Next time it'll last."

"Make it soon. I'm not getting any younger, y'know."

He smiled. "You're young enough."

He turned ready to leave and she reached over from the bed and slapped his butt.

"You take care of that for me," she said.

"Sure," he said.

It was love.

Midnight Companions

In the distance down Riverside a convoy of prowl cars spread from corner to corner and out of sight down the block. They could hear guns popping like a string of firecrackers and muted howls and screams. They hurried up 72nd like a pair of scared rats.

All Tom could think of was Andy.

That he'd left him again. Maybe for the last time.

Coward. Cheat.

Fool.

The first one was alone across the street near the pastry shop and she was so damn old and fat it was impossible to take her seriously at first, half running and half waddling across the street with her arms held out to them, the flabby flesh of her upper arms bouncing, fingers clutching like mottled claws.

By the time she stepped over the curb he had the tongs up. The old frail skull split open like a melon tossed in the gutter.

He felt his stomach heave. His legs felt rubbery. It was not the same as inside the bar. This was cold and brutal. This was execution.

He stared down at her.

"Easy," said Bailey.

He pulled him into the darkened doorway of a discount drug store.

There were four of them close by, all young girls — the oldest couldn't have been more than sixteen. They were dragging the man from the all-night deli out into the street, squealing delightedly as they threw him down over the double yellow line and two of them stepped on his hands while a third kicked him in the ribs and the fourth kicked his face.

They slid from one doorway to the next, stopping under the canopy of a restaurant. The restaurant was dark but it looked safe and there was a terrible urge to hide there, to simply get off the streets.

They moved to the lingerie boutique next door.

And they might have heard the women inside had not the pig-squeal screams of the man in the street become so horrible just then — because the women were making plenty of noise too. All the noise a dozen women can make in a riptide of destruction. They were tearing the place apart.

They watched through the broken window. The floor of the shop was a white ice-flow of silks and cottons ankle-deep under their feet, sparkling with broken glass. They'd torn down drawers and shelving and emptied it in heaps, hangers stripped clean dangling from empty racks like twisted mobiles, their shadows casting cobweb patterns across the walls while the women moved through the shop like savages at random forage, like violent children, tearing at the clothes as they put them on and tearing them again as they took them off, not a word passing between them as they reduced the store to rubble.

In the far left corner a fat woman in her housecoat sat on the floor, methodically tearing a green silk blouse to pieces. Next to her three younger women were trying on bras and nightgowns — but the bras were going on backwards and *over* the nightgowns instead of under them, and one of them had pulled on a sheer black camisole over that. Two teenagers stood naked in the middle of the store dismantling a mannequin.

Ladies' Night

A girl who was maybe seven or eight, her blonde hair in pigtails, her face made up like a Fellini whore, was trying to break through the glass countertop by lifting and dropping the cash register. She should not have been able to budge it.

Closest to them a woman in a red bodysuit with a black stocking pulled over her head like a mugger was stomping broken window-glass to bits beneath her naked feet.

"Christ," Tom whispered.

"Go," said Bailey.

They could not have been more than shadows out there but the woman in the bodysuit suddenly flung herself through the window and Tom lurched back into the gutter. He brought up the tongs. The woman grabbed them and he tried to wrench them free but the woman held on. He pulled forward and she fell to the sidewalk struggling like a fish on a hook. She would not let go.

"Tom! *Drop* it!" Bailey said.

He looked up and saw them moving slowly, purposefully through the broken display window like so many mechanical dolls, saw one of the teenage girls step over the rim of the window. He pulled at the tongs but the woman only slid along the sidewalk, red smears following her in two broad lines behind her bloody feet. The girl was out the window.

He dropped the tongs and ran, Bailey ahead. He looked over his shoulder.

The women followed.

They passed a pharmacy, 72nd Street Electronics, a hairstlist's. He heard only his own footfalls and Bailey's and those behind him.

A face peered suddenly through a restaurant window and he almost fell, he grabbed hold of a parking meter. The man's face pressed against the window bubbling a thick froth of blood and saliva. *Stay on your feet, goddammit,* he thought.

He ran and did not look back.

He saw that Bailey was hurting. He heard glass break again behind him and thought of the man in the window.

Across the street they were looting HMV Music, oblivious to Tom and Bailey. In front of the OTB he had to jump the body of a cop whose head dripped blood and brain-matter into the gutter. Another man lay beside him half on the sidewalk and half in the street. They turned the corner.

The newsstand by the subway station was on fire, flames painting Broadway a liquid red and gold.

"Got to stop," Bailey said.

Tom glanced over his shoulder. There was nobody behind them. Again he thought about the man in the window.

"Take it at a walk," he said.

The palm of his hand was throbbing. He could only imagine what Bailey was feeling.

They passed the jewelry store. The roller-skating shop.

"Oh shit," said Bailey. "Oh Jesus."

The corner of 71st Street was a battle-zone.

Men with bottles and broken chair legs and table legs were trying to stand their ground against dozens of women — mostly unarmed but formidable by sheer weight of number. Bodies littered the street.

It looked as though the men had been trying to break out of the bar on the corner. *You should have stayed put,* thought Tom. The bar had only two small windows and another on the door. It could be defended.

"Great. We got it on all sides now," said Bailey.

He turned. If it was the man at the window who had delayed them they were finished now, coming on fast behind them. Maybe a dozen.

"I can't keep running anyhow," said Bailey.

"What do you want to do?"

"Play any football?"

"Sure."

"How are you at breaking defensive lines?"

"How are you at parting the Red Sea?"

"We find the place they're weakest. Then we hit them. And it better be good because right now I got only one hit left in me."

They ran and coming up on them saw their opening, only five or six women near the corner of the building and three men holding them back and trying to work their way toward the basement-level door and back inside and they gave it full momentum, ramming hard from behind so that three of the women went down right away and Bailey whirled and slammed another in the chin.

Suddenly he was inside a tight circle of five and he and Bailey were enough to change the odds, moving toward the door as he kicked a woman in the shin and pushed her down, pushed another, grabbed yet another by her long blonde hair and flung her away into the crowd — and then they were tripping down the stairs into the bar and he was falling to the floor and the door was slamming shut the bolt ramming home and the room was filled with lights and they were not where he wanted to be not home at his apartment but they were not alone anymore.

"Good to see you. You were out for a minute there."

The big man was unsmiling, staring down at them with cool grey eyes.

"Thanks for the assist," he said.

He nodded, still trying to catch his breath.

He looked at over Bailey sitting beside him on the floor.

"Can you do anything for my buddy here? His shoulder's bad."

"You got that right," grunted Bailey.

"First aid kit behind the bar. Neil?"

"I got it." A dark, compact young man in a blue teeshirt hopped the bar.

He saw a dead woman lying across one of the tables. Another with a knife in her back sprawled along the floor. A third and fourth atop one another back in the restaurant area.

The windows at street level had already been covered by table-tops upended and nailed to the wall. That left only the smaller window in the basement-level door, too small to crawl through.

The table-tops were taking a pounding.

The ladies wanted in.

There were a dozen or so men in there, two of them working on the door, reinforcing it with crossbeams ripped from shelving and nailing them across the door. He looked at all the faces. The faces were scared. A few of the men were quietly drinking.

"Name's Phil," the big man said. "This used to be a bar. I used to own it. Now I don't know what the hell it is. I feel like I just survived the Alamo."

"Tom Braun."

"Bailey."

They shook hands.

The man in the blue teeshirt — Neil — came around the bar with a tackle-box, opened it, and started pulling out gauze pads, alcohol, peroxide and bandages. Bailey peeled off his bloody shirt.

"Christ, you need stitches. This is all we got."

"It'll have to do," said Bailey.

"I'm going to need some of that too," said Tom. He held out the palm of his hand It was still seeping blood.

"And a hefty scotch or something," said Bailey.

"Let's just say that what we have here's an open bar," Phil said. "Help yourselves."

A man in a v-neck sweater already had a bottle in his hand.

"Cutty?"

"Whatever."

The man turned over a pair of glasses and began to pour. His knuckles were bleeding and there was a two-inch gash on his left cheek.

They drank, sipping slowly while Neil worked first on Bailey's shoulder and then Tom's hand.

The pounding outside never let up for a second. The sound of it seemed to cut through his nerves like a buzzsaw — not just the pounding but the hissing, the moans, the growling, as though some evil alien fauna had collected out there and was calling to them, taunting them. *Come out and play. Come out and die.*

They heard gunshots and screams. No one spoke much.

"Why'd you try it?" Tom said. "Why'd you go out there?"

Phil shook his head. "We just got panicky I guess. We knew there were a lot of them but not *that* many. Damn fucking stupid thing to do. We just walked out into it. We figured, well, you know, they're women. So what. We took care of the ones in here okay."

"I guess you tried 911."

"You kidding? They had us on hold for half an hour, nothing but a tape saying all lines are busy and please hold. The emergency line for chrissake! I don't even think there's anybody *over* there."

"What the hell is happening?"

"I don't know. But I got a feeling it's happening all over the goddamn city. Jesus. Maybe all over the world."

"Anything on the radio?"

"No radio. Just a juke. Bunch of goddamn useless cd's. And they busted my tv."

He looked up and saw the shattered tube.

"Heaved a chair through it. Just about the first thing that went."

"I've got a problem, Phil," Tom said.

"What's that."

"I'm gonna have to go out into that again."

"Out there? Are you nuts?"

"I live three blocks down on 68th. My wife's there." He looked at Bailey. "With my son."

He watched the man's eyes and saw him comprehend.

"Jesus H. Jumping Christ."

He thought how Susan might already be lost to him — a thing like those outside. And he had to look away from the man's eyes then because the eyes seemed to accuse him. Or maybe he was accusing himself.

For all their bickering he realized he had never truly wanted an end to it with Susan but wanted only to turn the clock back to an earlier, simpler time. He'd been childish, selfish. And now there was so much that might never be said. So much left unpardoned and so many wounds.

Their years together seemed to dissolve as though they had no meaning. To pass on an evil wind.

"I need to get home to my son."

His fear for Andy's safety ran through him like poison. He knew it was possible — even, god help him, likely — that it was already too late, that he had not survived what Susan had almost certainly become. But if that was the case he still needed to know that, or he was going to go crazy not knowing. For that too he was guilty. He had no choice but to try.

"I don't know how the hell you're going to manage that, partner," the big man said.

"I don't either. But I can't stay."

He was aware that practically everybody in the place was listening. Bailey got up and hauled himself painfully over to the bar. He poured himself another scotch.

"I guess you'll need some company," he said.

"Not yours. Thanks — but not with that shoulder."

"The shoulder's done all right so far. It'll go three blocks more if it has to. You saved my life, asshole."

"I thought that was sort of mutual."

"Excuse me," said Phil. "But you got any idea how you're gonna do this? You remember what just *happened* out there?"

"Let's sit down a couple minutes and talk about it," said Bailey. "See what you did and *didn't* do last time. See what we can come up with."

The women were at the windows. Their fingernails raked the tabletops like someone clawing at the lid of a coffin.

The owner shrugged. "Sick of this place anyway," he said. "I been here all night. Maybe it's time I head on home."

The Dorset

There had been a fire in the Dorset Towers six months previously. An old woman was smoking a cigarette while cleaning out her clothes closet for the Salvation Army and dropped an ember into a pile of slips, bras and dresses. They began to burn. It was a small pile and consequently the fire too was small. But the old woman panicked at the sight of smoke and began to run — out into the empty corridor to the elevator and took the elevator eight stories down the lobby. By the time the doorman managed to break through her apartment door — the door had locked behind her and he'd neglected to bring his master key — the fire had spread to the living room, and by the time firemen arrived flames were shooting out her bedroom windows.

The apartment was gutted. But otherwise the only damage to the building was confined to the hall just outside her door, and that was mostly smoke-damage. Few flames had managed to crawl beyond the cinderblock cubicle and the sprinklers had taken care of those. To the apartments on either side no harm at all was done, not even smoke — so solidly was the Dorset constructed and so isolated was each apartment from every other.

At the time residents had cause to be happy with their building. Not now.

Many had already died so quietly that, standing in the hall, a passer-by might not have heard a sound. Not even as tables cracked under the weight of falling bodies or paintings came crashing off the walls or lamps or vases to the floor. Even the report of a .22 pistol was only a gentle *pop pop pop* as a woman on the nineteenth floor shot her entire sleeping family and then herself, splattering the foyer with brains and blood.

Fireproof, nearly soundproof, the Dorset became great a beehive necropolis in which no cubicle held any connection to the other except that death was present in almost every one like a worker at its grubs in a feast that lasted through the night.

Among the first to die was nice old Mr. Daniels, so well-loved by his wife that for supper this night of their thirtieth anniversary she had prepared his favorite meal — leg of lamb cooked Greek style, with oregano, mint and garlic. Never mind that the night was much too hot to have the oven on. Howard deserved it.

She had begun to serve it before the change came over her and she lost control of the knife.

She struggled against it — much harder than some of the others struggled. She loved him now just as she had so many years ago when he was a young career soldier and had saved her from the long winter of spinsterhood she already felt setting in.

There was a moment when she wavered, neither one woman nor the next, standing over him with the knife. Howard looked up and saw her struggle and the tears in her eyes and somehow comprehended and knew that something had happened immensely sad and horrible, that something had sucked her dry and left her dangerous — and more to prevent her than to save himself he reached for the knife.

It was too late. She was — and had been for many years now — much faster than him.

She neatly found the jugular. Mr. Daniels began to cough and shake his head, blood pulsing in tiny wavelets from his mouth as he tried to speak one last time and call her back to normalcy even as he died. Blood collected on the plate in front of him and sprayed the clean white tablecloth — and it was that field of red and white he saw last and the candles burning in celebration.

In apartment 1633 on the sixteenth floor Barbara Carroll, mousey-brown twenty-four-year-old wife to local TV anchorperson Dan Carroll, opened the screen to the nursery window.

Her husband, with two librium in him and having scored a good solid lunchtime fuck with one of the pages, slept soundly in the next room, the handsome blonde eminently archable eyebrows with which — even more than his voice — he delivered, impacted and inflected the nightly news, these famous eyebrows now impassive in repose. Three-month-old Linda Ann lay crying in her crib as she had for twenty minutes now, her diapers filled with sleep-dirt.

Barbara slipped the screen out of the window. She moved with difficulty — her body had never come back after the pregnancy. "Hush," she said and took the baby in her arms, her left hand gently patting the small pile of crap inside the diaper. The baby cried harder.

Barbara frowned. Linda Ann was already looking an awful lot like Dan.

She walked to the window. Sixteen stories down the streets were quiet. So much so that when she tossed the baby out the window she heard its wail for only three or four stories before it was drowned in silence.

She walked to their bedroom and watched Dan sleep a moment. Then she got a pair of scissors.

Never mind that her hands were shaking.

Those eyebrows needed trimming.

In the apartment above her a teenage boy was watching a rerun of *Happy Days* in the living room. The Fonz was showing uncommon nervousness about his debut as a rock 'n roll singer. He had just launched into a terrible rendition of *Heartbreak Hotel* when the boy's twin sister walked into the room and bashed him on the head with a cast-iron pan, still dripping water from the sink. His last thought was that this was ridiculous, she was taking their running nightly argument about who did the dishes far too fucking seriously . . .

Brian Campbell Risley, self-made home furnishings tycoon and womanizer was alive until 10:35 that evening.

Alive and happy — because it had taken nothing more than a dinner at Ginko Gardens to get the girl to go to bed with him, and Ginko Gardens was cheap. His bill with two drinks each was under fifty dollars.

Hell, the worst whore in town charged that much for a blow job. And this was no whore, this was young and pretty and didn't seem to mind the yellowish cast to his skin or the slightly flabby belly.

He couldn't wait to tell the boys over at the World Cafe how he'd peeled her out of the Adidas Marathon Trainers and sweatsocks and the brown Gore-Tex warmup suit and pushed her onto the big double bed. Great tits. Great butt. Young and strong.

As it turned out, a bit too strong for Risley.

Because when she felt him start to come she moved her hands off his pale skinny ass to his neck and pressed her thumbs into his throat until his yellow face went blue and his tongue slid out to the tip of his chin and wagged there like a dog's.

Which she thought was appropriate for Risley.

The fire began a slightly after midnight on the 21st floor in the apartment right next to his — Carla Landru's apartment.

She had gone to bed at the usual time with the usual dose of Prozak but the drug wasn't working, she lay in bed with the headphones on listening to that old punk band The Clash (". . . *is the music calling for a river of blood . . ."*) because all the music sucked these days just like everything else sucked and she kept wondering if they'd given her the wrong thing down at the drugstore. She felt this tingling . . . you know, *down there* . . . and a dryness in her mouth and then a little later a kind of blank open feeling that did not remind her of the drug at all and then she thought of her parents.

She thought of her parents *fucking.*

YUK!

Then she thought of *fucking her parents.*

DOUBLE YUK!

She didn't even *like* her parents!

And then she had a fun idea. She took off the headphones and got out of bed, turned on the lights in her bedroom and then in the hall and in the living room, turned on every light she passed until she got to the kitchen, turned that on too and stood grinning in the doorway.

Two doors down the hall Abe and Dee Dee Landru lay asleep in the only room still dark in the apartment, tired after a long day of golf for Abe and poolside drinks for Dee Dee at their Club out on Long Island. Carla, who had elected to stay in town that day to see the new Mel Gibson movie with a couple of girlfriends, on the other hand had never felt so wide awake. That cool weird *blankness* made her feel all giddy and creepy. She liked it. A lot.

She opened the cabinet beneath the sink. She rummaged through the bottles of Drano and Fantastik and boxes of Brillo and cans of nails and paint cans until she found the plastic bottle.

Twilight Lamp Oil, it read.

She put it on the counter.

She took a couple of eight-ounce tumblers from the cabinet up top and filled them, found a pack of matches in the container on top of the fridge and put the matches in the pocket of her pink cotton nightdress. She picked up the coke glasses and walked into her parents' bedroom.

She didn't bother with the light.

Daddy was snoring. That made her smile.

It also made her smile to see them both sit bolt upright sputtering and cursing when she doused them with the cold oil and heard her mother squealing — and then to see their faces change when they smelled the oil.

She had some trouble with the match at first but only for a moment and they were still together when she tossed it — they always slept real close. And then the bed was burning and they started rolling and running around the room, knocking things over and burning other things and pretty soon there was more light in their bedroom than in any other room in the apartment.

And it *moved.*
And it screamed.
And it writhed across the floor.

Dan heard the fire-alarm go off at the desk.
But by then he was in the mail storage room in back with the door locked, hiding.
An hour earlier five teenage girls had entered through the revolving door. They walked right up to the desk where old Willie smiled and said can I help you? which was the last thing he ever said because one of them grabbed him by his black tie and pulled him forward over the counter while the girl beside her took a red fireman's ax out of her yellow plastic slicker and lopped off Willie's head in two strokes.
Dan was on his feet and into the package room before she could pry her ax free, thinking that his years of broken-field running from the Man as a no-good street kid were finally paying off and now he huddled in a corner close to the floor hugging the Louisville Slugger he guessed was supposed to be a present for some kid in the building and waited for the ax to come crashing through the door.
He wondered why it hadn't come but didn't wonder too hard, lest he bring it on.
He heard the front door open once after that and heard a lot of sirens on the street. And now he heard the fire alarm.
He held onto the bat and *stayed there.*

The front door opening had been Sam Hardin's whore.
She walked through the empty lobby past the rows of mirrors and took the elevator to the sixth floor.
At his door Dr. Hardin greeted her in the usual way — head bowed, properly subservient. She pushed past him into the room.
"Good evening, mistress."
She didn't reply. He followed her into the bedroom. She opened her leather briefcase. While she was doing that he stripped off his clothes. He wished she would give him permission to look at her. The cruel slit eyes, the naked contempt in her gorgeous face. When he looked at her face he saw himself as *she* saw him. *Human shit.*

Ladies' Night

She was a goddess.

The cliches were routine of course but he loved them anyway. She would strip to leather bra and panties, black boots and black lace stockings. He would lie face down on the bed and she would tie him to the wooden posts with leather cuffs and then she would get out the whips.

He would beg her not to use them. She would ask him if he had been bad and he would have to say — quite honestly — yes *I have, mistress,* describing what he'd done as she beat him. Bad thoughts about his younger, prettier patients. Hatred of his ex-wife and distant married daughter. Overchargings. Faulty examinations. Useless expensive tests. Some sins went back twenty years or more, never to be forgiven.

He wished she'd let him look at her though he knew what he would see. The long red hair — her pubic hair was red too, though lighter — the cold green eyes, the slim heavy-breasted body, pink tips of nipples pushing through the suck-holes in her leather bra, the strong jaw, the rouged lips he had never once been permitted to kiss.

It was natural that she should despise him. She was beautiful. He was an old mean man with breasts like a woman's, the hair on his chest a smoky grey. A fat mean man who was a bad doctor, a bad husband and a bad father.

A very bad boy indeed. He lay down on the bed.

"Over," she said.

That was something new.

She would change things slightly sometimes, just to keep him off balance. He didn't mind. As long as it wasn't *too* different. As long as he got to confess and he got his whipping.

She reached down to tie his feet to the bedposts and then over him to tie his hands and he stole a glimpse of her face. He couldn't help himself. But she didn't seem to care. The cold dead eyes looked down on him. Encouraged, emboldened, he moved his head up and took her nipple into his mouth like a child, tasted leather and salt flesh. She let him nurse, watching him strangely.

And then pulled back abruptly.

Expecting rage, he closed his eyes.

But nothing came.

When he opened them again she was tying the cord around his privates — the one she used sometimes to lead him around the floor like a puppy, lapping at her heels. She had never used the cord in bed before.

He wasn't sure he liked this game.

And it was his money.

"Mistress . . ." he said. "If you don't mind . . . I'd rather not . . ."

She looked at him once. Then laughed.

Then pulled the cord so hard he screamed.

And kept on pulling until he had to arch his back to lift himself off the bed to ease the strain on his genitals and he looked at her with astonishment and saw her reach behind her with the other hand — leaning back in order to do so, pulling at him even harder! *with no regard for him, her client, at all!* — and then it was not the usual riding crop in her hand but a cat 'o nine tails with brass studs and she was whipping him *across the face! where it would show!* And pulling, jerking at the cord until he felt the wetness spread beneath him and the blood slide down his face.

She stopped. He fell back to the bed, sweating and unable to speak, his old-man's smell filling the room.

He felt the thin light blade on him then and there was still enough of a doctor in him to know what she was doing. He felt the blade sink deep into the top of his left thigh, pull down across the femoral artery and slice through his genitals, withdrawing, its arc completed, at the top of his right thigh.

And somewhere inside all his screams he heard the wet bubbling sound from within and knew that everything was slipping out inside him, sliding out into the light of the bedroom, all the secrets inside and that she would see it all, finally.

He cried and felt an overwhelming shame.

Dreams

On the second floor Elizabeth slept, silent and peaceful.

The birch tree brushed her window, a gentle scratching sound against the screen. The fine brown ringlets of hair across her forehead stirred. Her naked back glowed in the streetlight. Her skin drank in the cooling breeze.

In the garden below Lydia, her mouth caked with her own and Sheldon's blood, stared up at the pale white glowing flesh of the tree and saw instead another tree in the yard of her childhood home in Morristown, New Jersey, a town she'd not revisited since she'd opened the bookstore.

She and her brother used to climb it. It was a beautiful tree. It almost made her want to cry.

She wondered if the branches would hold her.

Elizabeth slept.

Susan awoke from a dream in which her father, long dead, was giving a press conference.

He was telling reporters that yes, he knew his daughter was a homosexual but that she had committed no crime and he would support her completely during this her hour of need. Reporters scribbled in their pads. Behind them unnoticed on the lawn Susan lay in bed with her lover, a woman much younger than she but whose face she could not see because it was buried between her thighs. She and her lover were naked, writhing with passion. Her father looked young and stern and vigorous.

Then Tom was at the podium, telling reporters that in his opinion Susan ought to be walled up forever and fed through a slot in the door.

Period.

She got up and led her lover into a forest. Her lover's hands were tied behind her back. Susan kept pushing her until she found a suitable tree and then slung the rope she carried over the tree and the hangman's noose over the woman's head and began to hoist her up. Her lover's feet kicked as though she were trying to run and then began to twitch. She felt a sudden sadness.

She woke up thinking of Andy.

Her thinking was unstructured, without logic, but obsessive. Andy Andy and Andy again, his image, his name — a strange claustrophobic sense of him coming from deep inside her like a wound opening and closing, pulsing over her.

She got up and went to his room and stood silent at his bedside.

She knelt beside the bed and smelled the musty odor of sleep. She leaned forward, heart racing, something urgent and irresistible happening inside her — and only then, in the grip of it, knew why she'd come.

Her hands moved lightly, delicately over the small thin chest and arms and shoulders, his small tight musculature beneath the cotton pajamas.

He stirred but did not waken.

A cauldron shuddered within her. Inside it something rising.

Her fingers found his wrists and gripped them. His eyes flashed open. Hatred, hunger and something twisted but which was also love drew lines of fire through her veins. The ache inside was immense and horrible and bore his name.

Ladies' Night

A wash of tears quivered in her eyes.
His breath upon her face was a fluttering of wings.
She moved closer. Her pale lips parted.

Armaments

"Wait a minute," said Phil. "You're talking about the Dorset? Big fucking highrise over at 68th and Broadway?"

"That's right."

"You're gonna love this. I know a guy's got guns over there."

"What?"

"Sure. Real good friend of mine. Name's Glen Sharkey. You know him?"

"It's a big building."

"Glen's a retired cop, off the force maybe two years now. He's got a Colt .45 and a .22 something-or-other — guns aren't my specialty. But I've seen 'em both. Keeps 'em in his bedroom closet. Even if he's not there I know where to find them." The big man laughed and stepped behind the bar. "Hell, I've got his *keys* here! Glen drinks a little. I keep a set in case he gets forgetful."

He punched open the cash register and took a key out of the drawer and used it on a small metal box next to the register. There must have been a dozen sets of labeled keys in there. Evidently the cop was not Phil's only customer who drank a little.

He found the ones he wanted.

"Here we go," he said. "We're set."

"You mean you want to come along?"

"I guess we're *all* coming along, right? Just *listen* to that shit!"

The pounding was incessant now. Nails were coming loose all the time and had to be hammered back again.

Their armor was looking decidedly frail.

"Besides I *know* that place," said Phil. "It's built like a concrete bunker."

"He's right about that," said Tom. "Built it that way for fire. The only way into an apartment unless you can scale the side of a building is through the front door, reinforced steel and aluminum plated. Again because of fire. That way you don't need sprinklers."

"That leaves the problem of getting out of here," said Neil.

"Okay, let's see what we got," said Phil. "Knives in the kitchen. Plenty of bottles. Got three fire extinguishers, one here behind the bar and one in the kitchen and one in the basement. And I think I can get us out through that door now without a hitch."

"How?" said Bailey.

"I got the idea looking at the first-aid kit, the rolls of gauze there. Any of you guys do any cooking? Ever make anything *flambe?*"

No one answered.

"Okay. No cooks. But suppose we took some of these hundred-proof bottles of cognac, some one-ten green chartreuse, some one-oh-one Wild Turkey and one-fifty rum and Polish vodka. Suppose we put 'em in a pot filled with water and heated 'em, then stuffed their mouths with gauze. Wouldn't we have some kind of low-grade molotov cocktails we could brew up here?"

"Damn!" said Bailey.

"Throw the bottles at their feet," said Neil, "and point the extinguishers in their faces. They'd never know what hit 'em. We could do it."

"We're gonna do it," said Phil. "Let's go!"

Procedures

For Lederer it was a first. He'd never given chase to a squad car before. He'd never expected to. It was a new experience.

But tonight was a night of a lot of firsts.

He'd never shot a kid for instance. But the little girls were as bad as their mamas, he'd found that out the hard way stepping out into a pack of them and got a screwdriver stuck in his leg for his trouble. The wound was just a flesh-wound but when she'd raised it again going for his chest and the little girl beside her started swiping at him with the broken bottle he'd shot them both and got the hell back in the car before the rest of them could get into the act.

And now they were chasing a squad car.

It was nuts.

The car swung west on 46th, fishtailing like a sonovabitch. Horgan pulled them neatly around and gained on her a bit. Lederer sat with his .38 in his lap watching her long dark hair tossing in the wind through the open window, waiting for a halfway decent shot at her. He didn't have to worry about pedestrians because the streets were mostly deserted by now except for stragglers here and there who had not found shelter yet. Or women. And the women were all lethal anyway. So he wouldn't have minded one bit if he could have piled her into one of these storefronts here with a bullet in her damn skull.

They knew now that it was not going to go away, that the women infected were going to stay infected and that was that, that this was all some crazy Pentagon Vietnam old-boy gameplan to make war on men by making war on their women but which they'd never dared to use because they knew what the press would do with it, an airborne chemical poison, a psychosexual hormone cocktail for god's sake designed to drive them batshit and terminally homicidal, a final batch of which somebody had overlooked for years and decided to move through the city as fast as possible before the talking heads got wind of it, on its way to its allotted final resting place in the Atlantic, but it had not made it to the Atlantic, it had stopped right here.

There was nothing to do but ride it out and let it take its filthy course and come in with the troops as soon as possible. He understood that was being arranged.

Wonderful.

Meanwhile they were engaged in a holding action. The holding action had cost them cop after cop tonight. It was not going to cost them Lederer. He had Millie to think of for one thing. He was glad she was up there out of it.

Not like this one.

Mary Silver saw a tall black man in her headlights and thought, *Hitler. Hefner. Rape.*

She slowed the squad car a little so she could go after him on the sidewalk. Her headlights and fender were already splashed with blood. Mary smelled more on the way.

The man saw her coming much too late and went over the grille like an acrobat, like a tumbler, leg-bones turned to powder at mid-thigh. She felt the impact throughout her body and the sensation pleased her enormously. First the whack against the bumper, the slide across the hood, then the head-on crash through the windshield on the passenger side. The man stayed there too, his head halfway through the broken safety-glass, dripping blood on the dirty carpet.

She'd found the car at Lincoln Center. Its once uniformed passengers were lying in a steaming heap across the stone staircase leading to the fountain. They'd been doused with gasoline but that had already burned away and two large dogs were at the bodies. Mary avoided the dogs carefully and slipped inside the car. She dropped her knife out the window. She wouldn't be needing it now. The car was better.

She drove around the park and managed to hit three men in a group, laughing as they flew like bowling pins in front of her. She missed a fourth when he ran up on the grass into the trees. At Central Park South she saw a short fat man in front of the Plaza. His tuxedo had already been torn somehow and he was scared and running, probably running home, but when he saw the police car he stopped and Mary ran him over. She could still picture him alive and howling, pasted like a bug on the sidewalk, as she drove away.

She proceeded down Fifth Avenue, and that was where the second squad car started following her.

She didn't mind. Company was okay too.

Lederer saw her hit the black man but there was nothing they could do to stop it. By the time she picked up speed again they were almost abreast of her. He got off a shot at her. Horgan kept on her good and tight. She skirted a cab, grazed a hydrant. At Broadway she turned south so that now there was room for them to pull up next to her on the right. He squeezed off two rounds and saw one of them clip the inside driver-side door. Almost, but no cigar.

Her car was swinging wildly now as though the woman were losing control but she kept it on the street at least, and Horgan was keeping up with her. The black guy on her hood stayed with her too, his right arm swinging up and down like Gregory Peck's on the back of the whale at the end of *Moby Dick*. It was dead weight keeping him up there — that and his head lodged in the fucking windshield.

At 42nd she turned west again, tires screeching. *Come on,* he thought, *make a mistake. We almost got you.* But then he and the woman must have seen the guy in front of the Lyric at exactly the same time because he knew she was going to swerve over in their direction and go after him way before it happened and he yelled *look out!* as the front fender glided toward them.

Horgan was good. But nobody was *that* good. She slid them off the road and over the curb at maybe fifty miles an hour into the plate-glass window of the porn-shop next to the Lyric and when he opened his eyes again he saw S/M magazines and lesbo and kiddie porn lying all over the floor and the hood of the car was plowed through a glass case full of dildos and fuck movies and the handcuffs in his lap were not his own but had slipped off a rack that lay broken and leaning against the passenger-side door.

There were two trophies on her prowl car now. This newest could not have been more than eighteen. He'd jumped the wrong way — exactly the way Mary was turning. When she hit him she was doing sixty and his body lay wedged between the hood and the fender like a foot-long hot dog on a steaming bun.

That made Mary cackle.

She kept on driving.

Breakout

"I want to see all you guys back in here Friday night," said Phil. "You hear me? Drinks are on the house."

Fourteen men would be a lot of drinks but Tom had a bad feeling that not all of them would be taking him up on that.

The eight-inch stainless steel carving knife felt oddly insubstantial in his hands.

He tucked it into his belt.

"We ready?"

Nobody's ready, thought Tom. We're going anyway.

Phil set one of the fire extinguishers behind him on the bar. He took the hammer out of his belt where he'd put it next to the knife and went to work with the claw on the crossbeams over the door.

They could hear them massing out there — *how many?* — moving off the windows to the door, attracted to the sound of breaking wood, concentrating on that now. Pounding, scratching.

He pulled off the last of the beams and used the hammer to loosen the pins on the hinges. Tom went to the locks, setting his extinguisher off to one side behind him.

The door would fall inward. They couldn't help that but they could see to it that it fell as straight and clean as possible into the room.

They had cleared a twelve-foot area in front of the door, pushed back the juke and the barstools, so that now all that remained there were the two big steaming pots which had just come out of the kitchen. The pots were filled with open bottles stuffed with gauze and rags. The men stood around them armed with knives and cleavers and broken table legs, whatever they could find, each of them carrying a dishrag against the heat from the bottles, and lighters or matches.

The younger man, Neil, stood directly in front of the door a few feet back with the third extinguisher ready. Bailey stood right behind him.

It felt like nobody was breathing.

Phil nodded.

He pulled the bottom pin on the hinges while Tom threw the slip-bolt and then the top pin as Tom threw the second lock and the door fell forward just inches from where Neil stood rigid as a stone with the extinguisher. Phil was already standing over the first of two women who had pitched through the doorway. The big man's hammer had come down hard across her head. At the same time Neil stepped forward over the fallen door, Bailey right behind him. He heard the sudden rush of air from Neil's extinguisher clearing the women off the stairwell followed by the sound of breaking glass as Bailey pitched the first bottle into the shadowy forms out on the sidewalk. By then Tom was already bent over the second woman, the heavy blade falling like a hatchet on her neck. Blood spurted across his thighs.

He stood up as Neil pressed forward, a cloud of white powder spreading out ahead of him. The women in the stairwell fell away, tumbling over one another. More bottles exploded. Then Phil was beside him with his own extinguisher and Tom was moving too, hauling the third up off the floor and pointing it, pulling the pin and pressing down the handle, and they were up the stairs in an instant, Bailey and the others right behind, moving up to the sidewalk and the street.

My god! There were *dozens* of them!

Ladies' Night

They had broken the streetlight and in the grey semi-darkness they swarmed around the tight wedge the three of them made and Tom knew the extinguishers wouldn't hold them long. Most of the men were outside, bottles popping on the sidewalk like firecrackers. He saw ghostly blue-yellow flames crawl the curbside, saw one woman fall screaming, her light summer dress on fire, saw a hydrant glowing and flickering in front of him as though coated with St. Elmo's fire.

A fat dark girl in jeans and sweatshirt was moving toward him with what looked like a torn-up parking meter raised over her head and he sprayed her but it did no good, she just squinted and kept on coming. He turned the tank in his hands and pushed it into her face, saw the nose and mouth seem to burst and the girl fall away. He turned and two more were coming at him. He sprayed them with the powder and they screamed and ran, hands clawing at their eyes.

Men were breaking for the street, trying to find paths through the crowd of women as they stepped away to avoid the flickering flames. Bailey was almost free, nearly to the edge of a shifting knot of women. Tom saw the table leg in his hands rise and fall twice and thought, *run, yes you've got the chance now* but Bailey didn't run. He turned and launched himself at them from behind, working his way back to Tom, busting heads. *You're crazy,* he thought.

He tried to keep moving steadily forward and out in Bailey's direction. Phil and Neil were both to the right of him and he knew there were other men who were still trapped behind him. Phil's tank was suddenly empty. He saw him swing it like a sledgehammer into the body of a teenage girl, cracking her ribs so that she coughed up blood as she fell.

An old woman was running toward him with a raised pewter candlestick in her hand. He pointed the spray into her open mouth and eyes.

Behind her a man lurched through the crowd, the blade of a knife protruding from his chest from behind the shoulder, his black teeshirt glistening, then disappearing into the flailing hands and bodies of four young women. He saw another man take a blow across the genitals from a cop's nightstick. A third man stabbed in the cheek.

Beside him Neil screamed. Tom whirled.

The woman held a claw hammer just like Phil's and Neil was on his knees. There was blood and two deep gouges the claw had made across his cheek and forehead. A second woman reached into his hair and pulled back his head. She was trying to scalp him.

With a paring knife.

He let loose a jet of powder but it was too little too late and the hammer came whipping at Neil sidearm. It fell across his throat and Tom heard it smash his larynx.

His extinguisher sputtered empty.

He went after her anyway, pulling the knife out of his belt and stepping across a line of blue fire on the sidewalk. He slashed at her and she ran, pushing two more women away from her on either side, opening a space in the crowd as she did — so that now Bailey was standing right there in front of him just a few feet away. There was only one woman left between them and Tom rammed his empty tank into the back of her head.

He tapped Phil on the shoulder.

They slashed their way to the street.

He didn't know anymore where he struck or what he hit. He swung almost blindly, trying not to fall amid the sprawl of bodies all around, slashing with the knife and feeling the deadness taking hold of his arm and the sudden shock running through it each time he struck, the warm rain of blood spilling over his hands and wrists and spraying fine mists across his cheeks.

And then suddenly they were free.

A car lay toppled on its side in front of the Savings Bank across the street. They hid behind it panting, trying to catch their breath. A short bearded man in a bloodstained white shirt broke through. They took the risk of being noticed and stood and waved him over. He was carrying a cleaver that had seen some use.

In front of the bar Tom counted four men left out of the original fourteen. He saw them moving in the shadows, heard screams and cries.

One bolted away up Broadway.

That left three.

They'd lost almost half their number.

"Dammit," Phil said.

"We can't help them," said Bailey. "They'll get out of this or else they won't. Let's keep moving."

He was holding the table leg away from him at an odd angle. Tom saw why. The wood was dripping with blood, slippery from top to bottom — and he remembered Bailey's mad charge toward him through the crowd.

"You're some piece of work," he said.

Bailey grinned. "I never said I wasn't."

They turned and looked down Broadway.

A lone figure stood under a streetlight about a block away.

Otherwise it was clear.

"Let's go," Phil said.

They moved slowly. The picture windows in both the furniture store and the lighting store had been knocked out and there was glass all over the sidewalk out to the street. It was impossible to avoid. It crunched underfoot, disturbingly loud.

They kept to the shadows close to the building.

There was a police car over the curb with a body dangling out the back seat — a black man in handcuffs, some poor bastard who never made it to the station. They found one of the cops a few feet in front of the car with his nightstick gone and his holster empty, a bullet in his brain. They never did find his partner.

Parking meters were broken away. A hydrant was spewing water. The place had the kind of bombed-out look you see after a hurricane without any time for cleanup. Inside the ruined lighting store the naked body of a little girl who could not have been more than four or five was lying on a chrome and glass table under a Picasso print like some sort of sick evil sacrifice to the modernist age. A man's bloody arm hung out over the windowframe. He'd been strangled by a lamp cord.

Across the street there was a light on in the florist's and they heard laughter from inside. Far away they heard glass breaking and police sirens. It was good to know the police were somewhere. *Live* police. He could have used a little law and order right now.

The entrance to the Burnside, so busy a few hours ago, was silent.

He wondered how the party'd gone.

He and Bailey peered around the corner.

A doorman was wedged inside the revolving door.

The entrance was brightly lit, open to view from both Broadway and Amsterdam. The florist's shop was right across the street. They were going to be damn visible. They paused in the shadows beside the overgrown jungle of a garden, undecided.

Bailey nodded toward the florist's shop.

"What do you think? You want to wait a while, see if they drift out of there?"

"I don't think so," Tom said.

He looked at Phil and the man with the beard. They nodded.

"Okay. Let's go."

Bailey turned. And for just a moment his back was fully to the garden.

She came out of a tree.

They heard it rustle and Bailey whirled but he wasn't as fast as gravity, she was on his back in an instant and the knife went into his neck just under his right ear, pulled swiftly across the right carotid artery and the cartilage of his adam's apple and the left carotid and out the other side so that what they saw was a thin line of blood moving along behind the knife which began to spurt and then pour out of him in a wide sluice right to left and back again, the woman toppling him to the sidewalk and holding on to him and pulling back so that the wound opened further and washed them all in a great hot spill of gore.

Tom tasted it in his mouth.

Bailey's blood.

He tasted Bailey's blood as Phil stepped past him and brought down his hammer on the woman's skull so hard he had to pull it free of her. She fell to the side and shook herself like a wet dog. Then lunged at him with the knife.

As though he hadn't hit her at all.

And then it was suddenly as though something *pushed* them. All three of them.

Some inner signal thrumming inside made wholly of violence pouring through them like an ecstatic bile and they went at her all at once, Tom screaming heedless of the women across the street inside the shop and staring at the cords of tension in her neck while he pounded her face with his fist wrapped tight around the handle of the knife its blade pointed up flashing in the moonlight and then kicking her while the man in with the beard chopped two-handed at her back hacking at her vertebrae with the cleaver in one hand and Bailey's table-leg in the other while Phil saw her knife clatter to the sidewalk to the glass from the broken plate glass window and stepped on the hand that had held the knife and thrust it into Bailey and ground the hand into the sidewalk into the glass until the fingernails popped while he pounded her head with the hammer.

They looked up from her twisted body flowing its juices into the littered black gutter.

Had they been attacked then it was possible they would not have had the will or strength to run, that they'd have died like hamstrung cattle pulled down by wolves, without fear or passion, too stupefied to care, more dead than alive.

The street, the sidewalk seemed to drain them like a tap on a dying battery. They stood in the same light they had feared a moment ago and felt nothing.

They looked in each others' faces.

The moment washed through them and was gone.

Goodbye, my friend, he thought.

I'll get them for you. As many as I can.

And I'll get *her.*

For the first time in his life he felt the depth of the cruelty inside him undiluted by guilt or fear or any other emotion and he did not dislike the feeling. He did not know why he should be focused so furiously now on Susan. He did not know why he blamed her. He knew nothing of her yet.

But it was as though she had brought them here. In a way she had.

"Come on," he said.

Wake-Up Calls

Lydia crouched in the treetop. The girl was sleeping and her back was naked. The sight of her nudity pleased Lydia the way the sight of her own body never had. She knew what she wished to do.

She was patient. She waited for the wind to rise or the sounds of the city to mask the sound the screen would make when she slid it open and climbed inside.

Gunfire sputtered a few blocks over. A siren whined. It was enough. Her hands went to the window and lifted it an inch. She pushed the sliding screen together and lifted it away. It made only a slight metallic rustling sound when she dropped it into the hedges below. Her fingers gripped the windowpane.

She stepped inside.

His mother lay across his body, her fingers like cold bands of steel over his wrists.

His mother's breath was his breath.

Her tongue was in his mouth.

It dripped poison into his mouth and Andy tossed his head against the pillow, dislodging her but the face would not go away, it followed him, its mouth open. He tried to free his hands but he couldn't. She tightened her grip and he felt like his wrists would snap. He struggled, felt silky breastflesh pressed soft against him beneath the sheer parted nightgown, her hips grinding.

It was not his mother. His mother was gone.

She was there instead.

He wanted to cry.

But there was anger there too because of what *she* had done to his mother and he tried to free one leg from under her, move it out from under and get some leverage. *Get her off.*

He couldn't.

She had him.

Her mouth sought him. He tossed his head and screamed.

"Get off me! Get off!"

Her breath was foul. He thought he was going to vomit. In a panic he lurched side to side trying to shake her, to buck and kick and fight her — and this squall-burst of movement on the bed jarred her away for just an instant, only an inch or two but enough for him to bring up his knee under and into her, *into her there.*

She howled and let go of one of his arms and slapped him hard. *Twice three times four* but that was okay because that meant his own arm was free too now and he balled up a fist and hit her in the face with everything he had.

She screeched like a cat and sat away from him and brought her hands to her face, releasing him, and he saw he'd made her nose bleed, she was wiping it and looking at the blood unbelievingly with wide strange eyes and he sat up and pounded at the face with both his hands as hard as he could — and somehow he was strong enough or crazy enough because she fell off him to one side. In a split second he was off the bed and scrambling for the open door.

He took one long running step and then another. He felt a hand clamp over his ankle and tripped and hit the floor head first, the right side of his face smacking against the floorboards, the air whooshing out of him. Everything went yellow and black. When he could see again she had the ankle in that impossibly strong grip of hers and she was dragging him like a sack into the living room.

He saw her glaring face and *knew* — knew better than he'd ever known anything in his life — that she was going to kill him.

His mother. This person who had been his mother was going to kill him.

The thought was so enormous it stunned him.

She was going to hurt him so bad that he wouldn't be there anymore. He would be . . . *nothing at all.*

And then he was crying, pleading, he didn't know *what* he was saying except that he was trying to get her not to kill him, to let him be. He was calling her mommy mommy mommy whining like a puking little kid eyes streaming tears nose dripping but he was so scared he didn't care, he couldn't care.

And she looked at him. Just looked.

Like he was so much garbage bagged and ready.

Like he was *already* nothing.

And maybe he was.

Daddy, he thought. Daddy please.

Inside Out

At first they thought the voices and the now-familiar sounds of breakage came from the florist's shop half a block away. But no. Someone was inside one of the darkened shops just across the street — the Korean vegetable market, the beauty shop, the tv repair, the meat market, maybe even the Food Emporium though the lights were on in there and they could see no one. They listened trying to pinpoint the sounds but there was a good breeze blowing again and you couldn't be sure.

They were almost at the corner. Anxiety tightened in his chest. They were really only yards away from Andy and Susan now. He could not help thinking — almost *knowing* — that the boy was still alive. What was left of his faith he put there — that somehow he'd avoided her. That he was waiting.

What about Elizabeth? he thought.

He felt a pang of regret. He had desired Elizabeth, yes, but he'd also honestly liked her. For a moment he wondered if they'd ever have gotten together — and if they had, if it would have worked. He guessed they'd never know.

On the south side of 68th Street, in front of a bank, a woman stepped out of the shadows.

She stood staring at them, her face a pale blank mask, her red cotton dress billowing in the breeze. She began to whimper. Her face began crumble with what seemed like relief.

And then she started to run, arms held wide to them imploringly.

It shocked him. She was crying, tears bright on her cheeks. *She's okay!* he thought. *How can that be? How can she not be one of them?*

He suddenly remembered the little girl lying beneath the Picasso print in the lighting shop. It hadn't really registered before — there were so many dead, so many bodies — but she hadn't looked changed. She'd looked murdered. Period.

It threw all his thinking into question. He'd been ready to kill Susan and Elizabeth too if he had to. But maybe some of them were still okay. Maybe Susan was okay. He pictured them hiding together, Susan and Andy, huddled safely in the darkness of their bedroom.

He glanced at Phil and the other man. *They see it too,* he thought. Amazing.

The woman was halfway across the street. She was sobbing loudly.

The man in the white shirt reached out to her. "It's okay, lady," he whispered. "Quiet down now. You got to be quiet."

The woman was maybe twenty-three or twenty-four, attractive in a way, very small and slightly on the heavy side. She wrapped her arms around the man and hugged him tight.

"You all right?" he asked.

She nodded, sniffling. The man turned to Phil and smiled. "Unbelievable, huh?"

"We better get going. Can you travel?"

The woman didn't answer. She just hugged the man tighter and Tom could see his face begin to change.

The man put his hands to her shoulders and gently began to push free of her but like the rest of them she was fast. When her head came up from his chest she was snarling like an animal.

Ladies' Night

She was shorter than he was so she didn't try for the neck — so that it was the *sound* of what she did that was so horrible, not the actual damage, the sound of her teeth clamping down on his collarbone grinding through shirt and flesh and scraping the bone as the man tried to throw her off, too shocked even to scream at first, gasping. But then she burrowed deeper and he screamed long and loud.

She clung like a leech and by the time they pulled her off him the women were everywhere all across the street.

They had been playing in the dark.

They came out of the beauty shop and they still had curlers in their hair some of them and one still had a mudpack on her face and a little pink sheet tied around her neck. A shopping cart sailed out of the Food Emporium heaped with steaks and roasts and sausages, a woman running behind it. A black woman with a Sony portable cassette player on her shoulder came running out of the tv shop.

It was the ones from the meat market who were the worst.

They carried things that glinted in the streetlight.

Phil had the woman by the hair but she clung to the man's collarbone like a bulldog so he reached into his belt for the knife and shoved it through the soft part of her neck just under the chin. The jaws opened. The woman spun away pumping blood over the sidewalk.

And then he had to turn away and run because they were on them from across the street and Tom saw the man's white shirt go suddenly awash with blood, the point of a long steel sharpener protruding from just beneath his breastbone. She had it in him up to the handguard and the woman was big and heavy and she lifted him off the ground with the thrust of it and then dropped him and then there were half a dozen of them crowded around him tearing.

They broke for the Dorset. They heard his screams.

At the entrance Tom flung open the nearest door and they raced inside. They turned and both their knives were up and ready when the first of them came hurtling through the door. Tom slashed her from eyebrow to chin and she went down and Phil put his knife into the second one's ribs. Two more came through the door on the far side of the lobby, one of them the big black woman with the cassette player blaring gangsta rap. The other was a svelte blonde jogger with a carving knife.

123

They stepped out to meet them as a third came through the door they'd just abandoned and Tom thanked god that she was just running at him crazy and empty-handed, because all he had to do was turn and hold out the knife and let her flaccid, naked stomach impale itself on the blade. She sank to the floor.

The music got suddenly louder and he felt something crack against the side of his head and a damp coldness as he fell and heard the radio crash down beside him, silent.

The woman whose face he'd cut was holding onto his ankle and hauling herself toward him across the floor, her blood-trail glistening on the maroon carpet. The black woman stood over him, giggling. In another world entirely she'd have had a good smile.

He struggled to his knees. His head was filled with lights. He hacked at the woman on his ankle blindly. He blinked and shook his head and when his vision cleared he saw Phil and the jogger circling each other warily with knives drawn.

They can even be careful, he thought.

The black woman stooped to pick up the radio. The woman at his ankle was dead, her head lying in a widening pool of blood.

He tried to get up but it was impossible, he was too dizzy. He fell to his hands and knees.

He looked at the black woman as she raised the radio over her head. He heard the static crackle. *I'm going to be killed by a fat lady,* he thought. There wasn't a thing he could do about it. The radio was poised above her head and he bowed his own to receive it like a good bull taking his coup de grace, thinking *I'm sorry Andy but god I tried* and then suddenly he heard a loud *crack,* looked up and saw the woman's head dart off to the right as though jerked by a rope, her feet rising up off the ground, her body falling like a sack of lead.

He stared down at her in amazement. Her head was a shattered mess lolling on her neck. He looked up and his eyes slowly focused on the black man standing next to him.

Dan. His Louisville Slugger on his shoulder like he was waiting for another pitch.

The other pitch was the jogger.

She'd backed Phil up to the door by now and somewhere along the way she'd stabbed him in the shoulder. She saw Dan coming and tried to move away but there was nowhere for her to go. The desk was right behind her — old Willie, the deskman, headless, seeming to reach out for her with both hands.

Dan walked over to her as confidently as you would swat a fly. He swung the bat one-handed at her midsection.

She put her hands out to block the blow and he heard wrists and fingerbones shatter. The knife spun away to the carpet.

Dan let the bat drift back behind him slowly, taking his time, placing the shot. The woman tried to raise her broken hands to protect herself. He swung the bat and hit her full in the face. The head whipped back. The face exploded. She sunk to the carpet.

Dan examined the bat.

He flicked two front teeth out of the wood with the tip of his finger.

"Damn! It's good to see you, Mr. Braun. You all right?"

Dan helped him to his feet.

"I was hoping you were cops," he said.

"You see Susan or Andy tonight?"

"Nope."

"You know Glen Sharkey?"

"Tenth floor? Sure?"

"He's got guns up there," said Phil.

"No shit."

"First Andy," said Tom, "then the guns."

"You sure you don't want to think about that?" Phil said.

"What would you do."

He moved Phil's hand off the shoulder wound. There was a lot of blood. The cut looked deep.

"You up for this?"

"Tear up some of this shirt for me and tie it off. Then we'll go and get your boy."

Tom ripped Phil's shirtsleeve to the shoulder and tied it off just above the wound. He'd been right — it *was* deep. But at least she hadn't hit an artery.

"I'd rather not trust the elevators. Let's take the stairs," he said.

They walked past the first bank of mirrors to the stairwell door.

Tom opened it carefully and looked inside. It was clear. He turned to Dan and Phil and glimpsed the three of them reflected in the mirror behind them. In the harsh overhead light they looked like ghosts. Bloodless, like dead things.

They hit the stairs.

Elizabeth Has a Visitor . . .

Clarity had come immediately and with great force.

In the moment between awakening and her plunge off the bed she realized that the shape moving through the open window was a woman's, but that didn't matter in the slightest — she sensed the threat. Her dancer's body did not betray her. Her first leap off the bed took her halfway across the tiny studio apartment. She heard the bedsprings creak behind her beneath the woman's foot and heard the woman growl and by then she was at the door.

She'd double-locked it as always before she went to bed. With perfect economy of movement she threw the first lock and then the second and her hand was on the doorknob when the woman crossed the apartment from the bed to the door and slammed her from behind.

Cold damp hands fell across her naked shoulders and spun her around. She stared into its face, its lips split open in a dozen purulent lesions glistening pus and blood. The mouth from cheeks to chin was brown and cracked like dry mud. The eyes were rheumy yellow, not white, and shot with red.

The death mask that was Lydia smiled.

Her torn filthy shirt was unbuttoned to the waist. She felt cold soft breastflesh press against her own as the powerful arms wrapped tight around her back. The mouth drooled against her neck.

She lurched back against the door so that for a moment there was a tiny space between them and managed to wedge her forearms up into that space, moving them up over the clammy graveyard coldness of the woman's stomach and breasts, up to the collarbone, shaking herself violently and throwing herself back against the door while the woman clung to her, sucking at her neck, the lips pulling back and mouth opening to bite, her arms finally rising up over the woman's and then the elbows striking down hard against her forearms, breaking her hold.

The rest was instinctive.

Elizabeth went for the eyes.

Her fingers pushed deep and curled toward her. The woman screeched and jerked away, her own backward motion clawing the eyes from their sockets so that they hung down her cheeks from long umbilical tendrils, twitching as she backed away. Elizabeth watched her — astonished — stared as the woman groped for them wildly and felt her stomach heave as she saw her paw the left eye off her face and watched it roll across the floor trailing muscle fibre like a grisly ball of twine.

She flung open the door and ran out into the hall, screaming in horror and relief from horror, tears bursting from her eyes like blood from a punctured vein, stumbling toward the elevator doors. Her voice echoed down the long hallway.

It did not go unnoticed.

All along the corridor doors began to open.

And even through her panic she recognized some of them. Old Mrs. Strawn from 222 in housecoat and curlers, an ice-pick in her hand. The nurse in 226, Estha, in bloodsoaked camisole and tap pants. Two little girls she often saw playing in the lobby, one in powder-blue pajamas and the other naked, peering out the doorway of 228, both of them covered with blood from chin to chest.

Ladies' Night

For a moment it was impossible to comprehend. An intruder —
even *this* intruder — had been one thing. But this . . .

. . . she'd stepped into madness. She *knew* these people! These . . .

. . . *women. They were all women.*

Not a man among them.

Tom, she thought. *Andy.*

The Braun apartment was just next door.

The stewardess from 210 was moving toward her, naked except
for a pair of red silk panties. Her shoulders and upper arms were
scratched and bleeding.

Suddenly they seemed to be everywhere at once — in back and
in front of her, by the elevator, by the stairwell door. Some of them
nameless to her, strangers. Moving together with a slow confidence,
arms reaching out to her, a dense web of deadly power. Mrs. Lyons
almost near enough to touch, shuffling toward her, icepick rising.

Elizabeth shoved her aside and heard her hit the wall behind her.
She flung herself on Tom's door and pounded it with her fists.

"Tom! Andy! Sus . . . !"

She tried the doorknob. It was locked. She rammed it with her
shoulder.

"Tom!"

Her own apartment was cut off to her now. The stewardess was
blocking the way. The thing inside with the dangling eye would have
been infinitely preferable. She slammed at Tom's door.

"Please! Help me!"

A cold hand touched her naked thigh. She whirled.

She slapped the little girl's hands away in revulsion. Her sister was
beside her smiling, reaching for her, clotted blood smeared across her
pajamas. Behind them the others moved steadily forward. She shoved
the first girl back into the crowd, grabbed her sister's arm and flung
her into them too, but their combined weight was nothing. And when
they saw that she was going to fight they moved with lightening speed.

She darted to the right toward the stairwell door but they were on
her in an instant, hands reaching into her long hair and pulling her to
the floor. Suddenly they were everywhere — and she realized the full,
terrible implications of her nudity. The hands slid out of her hair and

raked long sharp fingernails across her cheek. Teeth sank deep into her thighs, her breasts, her belly. Old Mrs. Strawn's icepick thudded into the floor an inch away from her neck.

She flailed wildly, kicking, pushing them off her body. Powerful fingers gripped her arms and wrists and pinned them to the rough carpeting but her legs were free and she fought furiously, her ferocity surging.

She felt a pang of agony and saw the nurse's teeth sinking into her inner thigh. She closed her legs over the woman's neck, locked her ankles together and jerked them up and down once as hard as she could, heard the neck snap, and rolled the body away from her like a broken doll. She planted her feet flat on the floor and pushed up into a backward roll and kicked at the two women holding her arms, missed the stewardess on the left but caught the other woman square on the chin.

She exulted in it. She had one arm free again.

She rolled forward again and on the downswing her legs fell across the shoulders of a middle-aged woman and knocked her to the floor. She pivoted left and struck the stewardess twice in the mouth. The lip split but the woman held on. At the same time she felt someone bite deep into her side just above the hip but the arm had to be free never mind the teeth so she hit the stewardess again and kept hitting her until the hands dropped away, then turned and brought her elbow down across the neck of the woman at her side.

She sat up and pressed back against the wall and pushed herself to her feet.

The door to Tom's apartment opened.

She turned to run inside and saw Susan standing in the doorway.

Teeth grinding. Eyes rimmed red.

Smiling, stepping toward her.

She ran.

The stewardess was rising. Elizabeth rammed her and sent her flying across the hall, used the impact to spin herself toward the door to her own apartment She pulled the door open. An arm went around her neck and she turned inside it thinking fuck *you,* brought her knee up into the woman's stomach and heard the whoosh of air, broke free and stepped inside as the woman gripped the doorframe and Elizabeth slammed the door on her fingers, heard the shrill cry of agony with delicious satisfaction, opened the door and when the hand fell away slammed it again, threw both locks and turned around.

The woman's eye was still dangling.

She was down on the floor next to the bed, mewling like a cat, trying to find the other one.

"A little to your left," Elizabeth said.

She'd beaten them.

She walked around the woman to the open window and pushed it shut. She turned on the overhead light and went to the bathroom. She turned on that light too.

Her face in the mirror was bruised and scratched and dirty. The bite-marks were deepest on her thigh, her side, and her left breast high up near the shoulder. There was a surprising lack of serious bleeding.

She held the washcloth under the tap water and gently bathed the worst of it, smeared bacitracin into the wounds and then walked back into the living room.

The woman had found her missing eye. She was fumbling with it insanely, trying to find a way to put it back again.

Elizabeth took her nightgown off the chair and put it on.

The woman seemed to sense the angry force of her. She sobbed and scuttled closer to the bed.

On a shelf beside the window stood a large ming aurelia — her only potted plant. Elizabeth thought it was a shame to destroy it but whether from relief or fear she still was shaking uncontrollably, she needed to be calm and think and she could not do that with the woman there and she could not stand the mewling.

She wondered if Susan had killed Tom and Andy. My god.

The aurelia must have weighed thirty pounds. She lifted it carefully and moved over to the woman and let it drop.

The mewling sounds stopped.

She stared down at the woman's body and the scattered shards of pottery.

I'll have to clean this up, she thought. She guessed it could wait till morning.

Morning, she thought. *And then what?*
She shifted her gaze to the window. It was hard to think clearly.
She didn't know.

. . . While Andy Gets a Breather

A dull pain spread through his chest and throat, a lethargy in the pulse of his blood, a cold ache throbbing through his limbs. He was done with struggling. Her thumbs maintained a slow even pressure on his throat.

There was a strange little man hungry for air inside him and all he could do was to let the man die.

He knew she was enjoying it. How his tossing and squirming had run slowly down and then stopped. She was looking at his face, taking her time, her head tilted to one side watching him as though she were curious about something.

He saw colors dance before his eyes and despite the pain saw how pretty they were, the blues and greens and yellows. There was an empty feeling in his stomach.

He wondered how long it would take this way.

Probably so did she.

He didn't think it would be long now . . .

. . . and never knew that it was Elizabeth at the door who saved him.

Susan heard the pounding and the shouting, the commotion in the hall. Her fingers loosened slightly. She listened. Then more pounding and someone calling names that were familiar to her. She dropped the boy to the crimson persian carpet and went to the door . . .

. . . and his first breath of air was the most painful thing he'd ever felt in his life. It seemed to slide down his throat like a redhot poker. Even the awful wracking cough was a relief after that. He began to feel a tingling in his arms and legs, which amplified and distorted until his body seemed one great slab of pain.

He knew he had to get out of there. The physical SOS to that effect was overriding even his agony. He scrambled across the carpet into the bathroom, his breathing so loud to his own ears he was terrified she could hear him. Only when he got inside did it occur to him to wonder why she'd dumped him and how he'd got so lucky.

He locked the door.

To Susan the girl at the door was not Elizabeth. She was just a kill, someone who she clearly sensed was *not like them.* When the girl turned and eluded her she didn't mind. She quietly closed the door. And then went back to the other one.

Who was missing.

She looked in the kitchen. He wasn't there. She looked in the bedroom. He wasn't behind the bed or in the closet or hiding behind his dresser. She looked into her own room. He wasn't there either.

She began to laugh.

She knew where he was.

He was in the bathroom.

Washing his face. Taking a shower. Brushing his teeth. Shitting.

The bathroom door was locked and the light was on inside. She rattled the doorhandle. She heard a rustling sound and that made her laugh again because now there was no question that he was there and the door was flimsy, she could break it down easily. *Flimsy.* The word posted itself in her mind like an advertisement on a billboard. She looked at the door.

And then methodically began to kick it to pieces.

. . . And Daddy Gets a Gun

Halfway up the stairs they heard the screams and laughter and the sounds of struggle, of bodies falling and pounding into walls.

Goddammit! *Right in front of the fucking door!*

"Guns first," whispered Phil. "We got to change our plan here."

"Bullshit!"

"You love your son? You want to live to see him?"

"He's right, Mr. Braun."

"You assholes! That could be *Andy!*"

"Unh-unh, Mr. Braun. *Listen* to 'em. Could *Andy* put up a fight like that?"

Dan was right. It sounded like maybe a dozen out there. Whoever was behind that door was struggling hard to keep on living.

"Whoever it is, Jesus, we should help!" His voice sounded almost petulant to him.

"Hey. You can be a hero or you can save your son. *We need those guns,*" said Phil. "We can be back here in *minutes.*"

Tom knew they were making sense and he also knew he was verging on hysteria. He fought for control, trying not to fall apart right then and there in the stairwell. He wasn't going to be any goddamn help to Andy if they went out there and got themselves killed but to be this close was torture.

His connection to Andy was still alive and somehow he felt that that meant so was Andy.

"Okay," he said. "The elevators. It's faster."

They hurried back downstairs and hit the first floor landing at a run. Dan pushed open the door and they were out in the mirrored corridor and rounding the corner to the elevators when they saw the four young women in front of them. But by then they were moving fast and kept on moving, Phil taking one of them by the arm and stabbing her in the side then turning and hitting the call-button, Tom backing the second to the mirror so that he stared at his own hard eyes as he stabbed her in the stomach. Dan was wielding the baseball bat like a two-handed sword, the last two women falling in front of him like grass before a demented reaper. One of them scrambled away from him on her hands and knees with her skull bleeding and Tom thought that it was the first time he'd seen any of them show that kind of fear. It was almost human.

The door to the middle elevator opened and they swung inside. Tom hit the button for ten. The door slid shut and then there was nothing to do but wait while the elevator ascended. The very normalcy was oppressive. Here he was, doing the same thing he'd done a thousand times, staring at the imitation brass of the wall surface, listening to the hum of machinery, waiting.

Everything's normal but us and them, he thought. Just another little ride in the elevator. Sweat beaded Dan's forehead. The bat rested lightly on his shoulder. Phil's fingers opened and closed on the knife-handle. *Clubs and knives,* he thought. Back to basics.

They stepped out into the hall.

Apartment doors hung open all along it.

One had been pulled off its hinges and lay across the hallway.

Ladies' Night

There were traces of what looked like blood on its inner side. Garbage was strewn around — wrappers, cans, melon rinds. Near the elevator a section of wallpaper had been torn away, the pasteboard behind it bone-white. Someone had smeared the wall with excrement.

They turned the corner. In the laundry room — every floor had one — a man lay face-up in the first tumble drier. His eyes and mouth were open and his hands were folded in his lap and he was covered with soap powder. They'd drowned two men in the top-loader washers, one of them wearing a bathrobe and the other only a pair of boxer shorts.

They moved down the hall to Sharkey's apartment. Dan was ready with his passkey.

The door to 1034 was closed — *but not locked.*

Phil pushed it open.

They listened in silence.

He turned on the light in the living room and they walked inside.

They knew immediately there was no point calling for Sharkey. The smell was strong here, a salt-sweet reek and the smell of human wastes. They locked the door behind them and began to look for him.

The living room, dining area and kitchen were undisturbed. In the bedroom Phil went to the closet, reached up on to one of the shelves and removed a small pistol from beneath a pile of sweaters. Under another pile he found a box of shells. He felt around further.

"Shit, I can't find the Colt," he said. "Maybe he sold it." He loaded six bullets into the pistol and slipped the box into his pocket.

"Maybe he's got it on him," Tom said.

"Maybe."

"Mr. Braun?" said Dan. The black man was on his knees holding up the bedcovers which had dropped partly off the bed. The tip of the sheet was shit-stained and beneath the bed they could see a dark twisted form.

They pulled him out.

The face was bloated, blue and yellow. The belt from his bathrobe lay embedded in the swollen flesh of his neck and his fingers were frozen still clawing at it.

Phil looked down at him.

"Guy drank too much but he was never mean," he said. "It's a goddamn shame. You want to bet he figured he got lucky tonight? Nobody broke into this place. His door was open."

"Maybe that's where the Colt went."

"Maybe."

Dan patted the pockets of the bathrobe and peered beneath the bed. "He didn't have it on him," he said.

"Let's go," Phil said. "We got one gun. It'll have to do."

The elevator was still there open waiting for them. But this time there was nothing familiar-feeling about it. The air inside as they descended felt thick with a terrible promise. He heard a soft clicking sound and looked at Phil and saw him staring down at the gun and knew that he felt it too.

He'd just clicked off the safety.

Home Improvements

The lock was going to hold but the bathroom door was some sort of cheapjack plywood and Andy gave her two or three more kicks before she got inside.

"Noooo!" he moaned.

His voice sounded low and hoarse to him, like he'd grown five years in the last five minutes.

He pushed open the medicine cabinet. Most of the bottles were plastic. But there was a heavy jar of cold cream and some perfume and cologne bottles. She kicked the door again and he heard the panel shatter.

Behind the cologne he found his father's old straight razor. He opened it. He ran his thumb over the edge. It was stained and dirty but it was still pretty sharp.

The razor and the bathroom gave him an idea. The idea was right out of *Psycho* and it scared the hell out of him but she scared him more. He left the cold cream and perfumes in the sink and with the open razor in his hand slipped into the shower stall and threw the clear plastic curtain.

He could hear the door splinter.

He turned the shower on and threw the dial over to HOT as far as it would go, then quickly angled the shower-head away from him and stepped up on the ledge of the tub behind the spray.

The shower-head was already too hot to handle so he peeled off his pajama top and wrapped it around his hand.

Through the plastic curtain and the fog of steam he could see the hand moving through the hole in the panel fumbling for the lock then withdrawing. The door opening. His mother suddenly inside.

He wanted to scream but he held it in, tried to stay calm because he could not make any mistakes here, it had to be just right. He could hear the thunder of falling water. It burned his hand through the wet pajama top but he held onto the showerhead anyway, willing himself to not let go.

She drifted to him through the pluming mist of steam and threw the curtain.

He heard the sharp metallic sliding rip of the curtain-rings across the rod and jerked the shower-head up in her direction. The hot heavy spray hit her full in the chest and she threw up her hands. She backed to the wall opposite the sink but his spray could still reach her and he turned it on her.

He heard himself screaming, yelling in pure release, and followed her with the spray.

She began to twist and howl but he saw that she'd fixed his position now behind the spray and it was like they were connected, he knew what she was thinking, she was thinking that it would be an easy thing to face the pain for just a second and get to him, so he slipped off the ridge of the tub, scalding his own naked back in the process, and launched himself at her.

He cut her once, twice, a third time, felt the terrible resistance of flesh beneath the razor and felt the warm spray of red. He did not know where he hit her, only saw her fall back against the sink and stumble to her knees and he knew he should be staying there, standing there, standing over her, killing her with the razor now that he had the chance but he couldn't, the awful sounds, the feel of the razor when it cut, the terror was too much. It was like he was in a room with every black evil wicked thing in the world and some of it was him — some of it was him with the razor.

It seemed that one second he was still in the bathroom and the next he was at the front door pulling it open and then standing frozen there, looking at them milling through the hall by the elevators and the stairwell all the way down to Lizzy's apartment, turning with a quick terrible purpose when they saw him, snarling.

He slammed the door. Locked it.

His heart was roaring. *He was in hell now, it was all hell, the entire world, this was what it was, not like he'd read or seen in the movies but this, exactly this.*

He heard the shower die abruptly.

He had never known a silence so thick and filled with meaning.

He'd hurt her.

And now he'd pay.

She was coming to *make* him pay.

Calm down, he thought. You got to think.

He still had the razor but it was not going to be enough — not now, not after he had hurt her.

There were things in the kitchen.

As quietly as he could he went to the kitchen and closed the double louver doors behind him. There were no locks on the doors but they would give him an extra moment. The cleaver was on a peg on the wallboard. He took it down. The cast-iron pans frying pans were on the stove. The biggest was too heavy for him so he took the next biggest. He opened the cabinet and took out a stack of plates. *The good china.* He was making noise and she'd know exactly where he was but it didn't matter, she was going to find him anyhow.

He put the pan and cleaver next to him by the sink where he could grab them fast and took up the stack of dishes.

He put his back to the far wall and waited.

He saw a shadow through the louver doors.

The pause that followed lasted a billion billion years.

He felt a rush of terror tremble him like an electric jolt and the doors burst open.

She stood there dripping wet with her nightgown plastered to her body and he took in at once the damage he'd done. The red skin blistering across her arms and breasts, the bleeding lines across her hip and belly. But all of it was nothing. The force of her was stunning. The dishes felt puny and ridiculous in his hands.

He threw them anyway. She batted them away and they crashed on the floor and counter. He grabbed the cast iron pot by the handle and threw it underhand as hard as he could like he was pitching a softball and he was lucky, it caught her in the stomach and made her double up for a moment and he rushed her with the cleaver.

She saw it coming.

She backhanded him across the face and sent him sprawling against the wall. He sat there dazed, pain careering through his face and jaw, looked up through a film of tears and saw her advancing.

He slashed at her legs with the cleaver and felt it connect, *the resistance of meat,* and heard her howl. He got up moving faster than he would have ever thought it was possible for him to move but it was still no good.

He felt an immense bone-shaking blow to the back just above his shoulder and then a second lower down, cracking his ribs. All the breath went out of him in a sudden rush and he fell flat across the floor. The tears were pain-tears now and he blinked his eyes to clear them and saw her foot right in front of him and he brought the cleaver down.

She stepped away.

He heard low evil laughter.

Goddamn you! he thought and pain or no pain he rolled over on his side pushing outward and up from the wall and lunged at her with the cleaver — and if he lived forever he would never forget the sound of it.

Nor what he felt and saw.

The blade had all but disappeared into the flesh of her thigh and stopped against bone. He'd *heard* it stop. A huge flap of muscle and skin enveloped it. He saw muscles twitching, veins pumping bright hot blood. It sluiced over his hands still clutching the cleaver. He let go as though the handle were electrified.

She toppled over beside him and for a moment they were face to face and he stared into her red-rimmed eyes. And she opened her mouth wide and *roared* at him.

It was not his mother.

He stood and backed away, watching her agonized attempts to remove the blade, watched the hands go to the dripping handle and then fly away as the slightest touch drew her through infinite waves of pain, the face seeming to turn in upon itself, suddenly old, ancient, the mouth open sucking air and whimpering.

Not his mother.

A gruesome evil heap on the floor.

She was nothing.

He stooped and reached for the cast iron pan.

You've got no choice, he thought. The thing will get up again. In the movies they always do.

And you can't run away, you sure can't go outside.

He had no choice.

But suddenly he was sobbing like a baby.

He raised the pan high over his head and brought it down with all his strength.

And she was silent.

He ran to his bedroom and closed and locked the door and lay down carefully on his bed because his ribs throbbed terribly now. It didn't help that he couldn't seem to quit crying.

It was only a few moments later that he heard sounds from the kitchen.

The clatter of metal on the floor and a cry of pain.

The cleaver, he thought.

He heard a scraping sound, something moving through the hall. His ribs felt so bad he could hardly move.

And it wasn't over.

Redecorating

Mary didn't like it anymore.

The man on the hood of the prowl car.

The gleaming red face which dripped through the hole in the windshield onto the floormat. The arm that waved whenever she made a turn. He bothered her.

She stopped two blocks east of Grand Central Station, got out and walked to the front of the car and looked down at the second man, the one wedged between the grille and bumper. His head was gone. She had no idea when he'd lost it. The ragged flesh of his neck had turned black.

She grabbed him by the belt and tugged.

She got his legs down so that he was kneeling on the street, his arms and chest still stuck in there. His chest was soft when she reached in under him. She tossed the rest of him down and wiped her dripping hands on the pants-cuff of the man on the hood of her car. Then she grabbed his feet and pulled.

He immediately slid free. Almost free. Pieces of him still clung to the windshield. She pulled him across the hood. His head thumped down on the bumper. She threw him across the body of the first man and stood there breathing heavily for a moment, then walked over and sat inside the squad car.

She was feeling that tingling again.

She reached down and put her hand down there, and she was wet again too. She started the car and raced the motor.

She let the car idle a minute and threw it into DRIVE. The left side of the car rose slightly in front and then in back as it rolled over the pair of bodies. She cruised along slowly.

She kept one hand down inside her and the other on the wheel. Waves of pleasure rolled over her. She heard the siren wail behind her and pressed her foot down on the gas pedal and the car burst forward.

"You look like something out of *Playboy*," she said.

She drove one-handed through the dark sea of bodies that populated her memories.

Painted Lady

The thing at Elizabeth's feet lay motionless, its head covered with potting soil. She sat on the bed and stared at it a long time.

It looked ridiculous, really.

She stood and walked carefully around it and into the bathroom. She peeled off the nightgown and, for the third time in just a few minutes, began to bathe her wounds.

She was almost out of bacitracin.

She remembered that her mother had favored Mercurochrome.

She found an old half-empty bottle in the medicine cabinet. The orange lines on her cheeks made her look like an Indian in warpaint. There were teethmarks and scratches on her thighs, legs, breasts, and stomach. She dabbed them with Mercurochrome.

There were stripes all over her now.

She walked back into the living room. The body had not moved. Of course it hadn't. There were sounds coming from the Brauns' apartment next door but she barely registered them. She turned on the television. There was nothing but a lot of static. She turned it off again.

A dullness, a lethargy had settled in. As a dancer it was strange for her not to feel in touch with her body. But there was little sensation except for the throbbing of her wounds. Her arms felt weightless, the soles of her feet, numb. She realized she was naked.

Where had she left it? The nightgown?

She walked to the bathroom again and there it was on the floor. It was streaked with dry blood.

It wasn't what she wanted.

She'd get dressed instead.

She went to the closet and picked out a blue silk blouse and loose-fitting white linen pants. Soft against the wounds.

She put them on and thought, *what next?*

Everything tumbled in a gentle confusion.

She couldn't just sit there with that thing on the floor.

Her eyes kept returning to the window. Her thoughts seemed bound up in that cobalt sky. Dawn was arriving soon and the window beckoned.

The woman had come through the window.

She opened it an inch. She felt a cool breeze on her bare hands, felt it billow the blue silk blouse. *Sensation.* She opened it further and closed her eyes and let the breeze wash over her, felt it brush the skin of her throat and rustle her hair.

She heard screams from the street and simultaneously, laughter from the hallway. She slammed the window shut.

The woman had come through the window.

But if the woman had come in *that way, couldn't she go* out *that way?*

Sure she could. She could wait till dawn, look for a policeman or a man — *any* man — to walk by and call out to him below through the window and climb out onto the tree and escape. She only had to wait.

She sat down on the bed, willing the sky to brighten. *Soon,* she thought. She glanced at the thing on the floor in the ruins of her room and thought how it had not moved and now neither would she. She smiled.

We're two of a kind, she thought.

Close Range

At first there was nothing to it. The elevator doors slid open and the men moved swiftly down the corridor. The first thing they saw was the body of a woman with her neck broken lying on the floor. Then they saw the others. There were maybe twelve of them who had begun to drift back to their individual apartments and who were scattered throughout the hallway and now were turning slowly and deliberately like hunters scenting new game.

Phil started firing and the first to fall was old Mrs. Strawn because she was closest and held an icepick, the explosion in the middle of her blue housecoat shaking some of the curlers out of her hair as she dropped. The next was a young girl Tom didn't know, wearing pajamas, shot twice in the ribs.

By that time the others realized they had a problem here and started moving faster.

Dan stepped out three or four paces to the right of Phil and began working with the bat, cutting a path to Tom's door. Phil fired twice and a little naked girl went down beside him and a middle-aged woman fell to her knees clutching at her neck. Phil began reloading.

Tom stood ready with a knife in each hand but there wasn't any need. The bat was keeping them at bay. He watched three of them flee around the corner and recognized Mrs. Strawn's older sister — a carbon copy right down to the curlers except that the housecoat she wore was pink, not blue — waving an curling iron at him as she stumbled out of sight. A woman he knew to be a stewardess was backing away from Dan, who missed her once and then connected with her knee. When she fell to the carpeting he was on her with the bat like the bat was an axe and the woman was a log that needed splitting.

There were only two of them in sight by then and Phil had the gun reloaded. One was moving sadly, stupidly down the hall past Tom's door to the right where the hall dead-ended in front of the apartment next to Elizabeth's. Nowhere to go but straight to hell and that was where Phil put her. The other was just a teenager hissing and clawing at them with her back to the wall opposite. Phil walked in close and shot her execution-style in the forehead and she slid down the wall, her head bubbling a froth of blood.

They went to the door.

Phil reloaded the two empty chambers while Tom used his keys. The keys felt slimy in his sweaty fingers. The top lock was giving him trouble until he realized he was throwing it in the wrong direction, *Jesus,* it wasn't locked! it was only the bottom lock that'd been thrown. He slipped it out and fumbled through his keychain for the other one.

And that was when Mrs. Strawn's older sister stabbed him with her sister's icepick.

She came out of nowhere, moving faster than any old lady had a right to move and for a moment they'd let their guard down, Tom working with the keys, Phil reloading, Dan concentrating on Tom and the door that was going to open momentarily — and the icepick went into him at the collarbone near his shoulder and came out fast and down again into his neck and suddenly there was blood everywhere.

He felt no pain, just shock and fear that he was not going to make it, that he would never know what all the killing had been worth and what had happened to Andy. Andy, who had flogged him through a night of terror. The icepick slipped into him a third time — into his chest — as Phil fired directly into her face scattering blood and brains across the hall.

No, he thought. *It was not going to go down that way.* He pulled the icepick out of him and dropped it to the floor and stumbled to his knees.

He heard the echo of the pistol and then nothing, a vast empty silence. He struggled against a descending flood of color.

"Help me up."

He stared into Phil's eyes, read pity there. Read sadness. He focused on the eyes.

"Get me up."

They lifted him to his feet.

"Now. Give me the gun."

He saw them look at one another and knew what they were thinking. That it was crazy to give him the gun. He was probably a dead man already. But it was his son in there and his wife and it was his battle. He thought that as long as he could stand they couldn't refuse him. And he was standing.

"Please," he said.

He needed to dismiss the pain, the sense of something slowly trickling away. He put his back to the wall and held out his hand.

He felt them hesitate. Then heard Phil sigh.

The .22 didn't weigh much. He had that to be thankful for anyway.

He found the key on his chain and handed it to Dan, heard it in the lock.

The door swung open.

He moved inside ahead of them, the floor of his apartment bucking and rolling beneath his bloodsoaked shoes.

He willed away the mist.

The Family

Andy crouched behind his bed.

The forty-pound fiberglass bow was strung and a soft leather quiver of target arrows hung over his shoulder. He fixed an arrow to the bowstring.

Now, he thought. *Come on.*

There was an awful pain in his ribs but he didn't think pain had messed up his judgment, he thought he'd got it right. As soon as he heard her moving in the kitchen he'd ducked out into the hallway and turned on the light. Then he'd turned off *his* light and left the bedroom door wide open. That way he'd see her framed in the door so he could make his shot but she couldn't see him — she wouldn't know where he was in there.

He'd seen it in the movies.

He knew he'd hurt her bad — that was what the rasping dragging sounds were about and why it was taking her so long and he just wished she'd hurry up before this trembling got to him. His ears were keyed to the sounds as though they were a part of him. She was only a few feet from the door when they stopped again.

Come *on.*

Suddenly he heard gunfire — a series of short rapid popping sounds and god! they startled him he was so much into to these other sounds *she* was making and he threw himself back against the wall and lost his grip on the bow and the arrow slid off the bowstring. He heard its wooden shaft and metal tip clatter to the floor. To be without the arrow even for a moment terrified him.

He groped beneath the bed. But it was dark, he couldn't see, his whole plan was backfiring on him now and he couldn't find it! It had rolled somewhere.

A sudden panic seized him.

He couldn't hear her anymore! There were more gunshots and shouts and screams coming from the hall and maybe that meant somebody was coming to get him but because of them he couldn't hear.

Where was she?

He looked up — it took all his nerve to do it — and the doorway was still empty, thank god. He could feel the hairs bristle at the back of his neck. Terror was robbing him of everything, of all his determination. He was nothing but a scared little kid all over again because he couldn't find the arrow and he couldn't hear her.

And then he almost laughed.

Because he had a whole *quiver* full of arrows right here on his shoulder. He heard more shots as he pulled one free and strung it, turning it to fit the notch to the bowstring, and went back to his crouch position behind the bed.

He'd get her.

He heard the dragging sounds over the others from the hall and knew she was very near him, just at the door, just bending to the open frame. In his mind he could almost see her. He felt a tightness grip his throat like an arid wind.

He heard more gunfire. His staring eyes blinked once.

And she was there.

Peering inside.

She stepped full into the doorway, her form in half-shadow, one eye gleaming.

He pulled back hard on the bowstring. The pull was heavy and it was hard to keep it steady but he knew he had to do it right this time, it had to be over. He saw something glint in the light from the hall. The cleaver — raised over her head, stained with her own blood.

If she can do that, he thought, *if she can pull it out of her and then come back here to use it on me* — my god! how could you fight something like that?

She was indestructible!

He suddenly saw himself lying flat on his bed while she cut off his arms and legs and piled them up beside him, saw the cleaver pass through his skull and face, cutting it in half, his dead eyes staring up at her from a dreadful new proximity.

The bowstring cut into his fingers. He pulled harder.

Steadied it. Aimed.

And released the arrow.

Vicious, she thought. Olly olly in free come out come out wherever you are hiding in the dark, vicious, peekaboo eyeseeyou. Yours something said but the voice so dim and the evil little thing that hurt her hiding in there in the dark so that she stumbled on the bad leg as she peeked into the room and shook her head, no, denying it, denying the voice.

How nice how good the evil cleaver.

Vicious.

She moved just as he fired, the arrow aimed for her heart rising at its predetermined angle with terrible swiftness in the small space between them and sinking deep into the red cold eye. Andy heard her scream, a throaty roar of perfect agony from deep within, like she was burning, and the impact drove her back against the wall so that he could see her in the light, the open running burn-wounds like patches of decay, the legs caked and clotted with blood, the deep meaty gash in her thigh.

He saw her twisted mouth fill with yellow bile like fast-flowing magma, and bright spouts of blood pouring from her eye.

He stood up, terrified and fascinated, thinking, *please, let her die now*. Please.

But she wouldn't.

With the cleaver still clutched in her hand she reached up to the shaft of the arrow and broke it in half midway down its length. He heard it snap and then his own wailing, his own screaming. She shook her head spraying the room and him with blood. She raised the cleaver and started for him.

He reached for another arrow inside the quiver, his fingers slipping on the shaft, slick with her blood — and he couldn't stop crying. He knew she could hear him and that the dark wouldn't help him if she did but he couldn't stop.

Suddenly the cleaver split the bed in front of him clear down to the box-spring. He threw himself against the wall. The arrow he'd half removed from the quiver fell to the floor.

She pulled the cleaver out of the mattress and he saw her wipe the blood from her one good eye, almost seeming to smile at him in the half-light. He reached for another arrow. He pulled it free.

There was no time to string it nor any distance now between them so he dropped the bow to the bed and held the arrow out in front of him with both hands. The arrow felt thin, fragile. He clung to its frailty.

She drew back, ready to split him this time.

"Andy!"

It seemed impossible but he heard it. Once and then again. Nearer.

"Andy!"

She heard it too. She turned her head and listened.

"Dad!" he screamed. "Here! Here!"

He saw her in profile for a moment, turning, the broken shaft of the arrow tilting, rising with the upward sweep of the cleaver and then her back was to him and she was poised to strike, down into the shadows at some creeping ghost moving low across the floor in front of her and thrusting something forward into her belly which exploded at her, bursting bits of flesh and bone toward Andy out through the back of her like a grisly sunshower.

He saw the cleaver come down and heard it strike. He reached for the bow on the bed, a sudden powerful hatred rising in him because *the gunshot had not killed her, the bitch, the bitch nothing could kill her, he would have to go on killing her forever.*

At her feet he saw his father fire again. She had buried the cleaver in the muscles of his chest and he could barely get the pistol up at all so that the shot went wild into the ceiling. He heard her wrench the cleaver free.

The gun dropped to the floor beside his father's hand . . .

. . . and Tom didn't care. Because he knew by then. There had been time enough to see the boy alive and then to kill her. He knew he'd killed her. He knew that Andy was alive. He would have wished to live long enough to touch him, he would have wished that very much, but he knew what he needed to know and he'd done what he could. For once . . .

. . . and Andy heard the muffled chopping sound as the cleaver split his father's skull.

He had the arrow fit to the bow-string and he fired into her back. At the same time he saw a black man's hand reach over his father's body and take the gun.

The bullet caught her in the chest and the arrow in the small of her back. She fell backwards onto the bed and he heard the arrow snap beneath her weight. A bright gaping wound seemed to spread itself slowly across the middle of her chest. He snatched another arrow out of his quiver. He knew she was dead but he did not feel safe and without the arrow it was not enough.

And he guessed it was not enough for the black man either because he saw him step over his father's body and fire pointblank into her open mouth.

The room was still.

He smelled gunpowder. He smelled blood. He recognized the black man as Dan the security guard. Another man he didn't know stepped into the room, looking ashen in the pale dawning light.

They looked at each another and no one made a sound.

Epilogue - Daylight

Dawn, thought Elizabeth. Oh yes.

The sky was a murky New York grey. The streets were quiet. The sounds next door had stopped.

A cop would be perfect now. *There's a body in my room, officer. Please check the people next door. Look for the boy. I haven't got the nerve.*

She opened the window. The morning air was cool, scented with burning.

She could probably use the hall now. Everything seemed quiet there too but she was not going to risk the hall. Not again.

The tree was very close to the window and the branches were thick enough to support her. She stood on the heating unit and put one a leg out and an arm and grabbed the tree. *There.* She stared back at her open window. She hugged the treetrunk, thinking of the woman lying on her floor, until the shivering stopped.

She let herself slowly down. I'm surprised someone hasn't tried to break in here before, she thought. It's not real hard.

The peat in the garden was wet with dew. She'd forgotten her shoes. There was broken glass on the sidewalk so she walked down the middle of 68th Street toward Broadway.

Bodies. Abandoned cars.

If there are police around, she thought, I'll find them at 72nd Street. There wasn't any traffic so she stayed in the middle of the street. It felt amazing to be able to do that — to walk down the middle of Broadway for god's sake in broad daylight. The city was empty.

Apart from the dead.

She tried not to look at the dead.

She would tell the police first about Tom and Andy. Get them to check. She hoped they were okay.

The sky was brightening. I wonder if anybody can see that I'm not wearing panties under these pants, she thought. She'd forgotten them like she'd forgotten the shoes. I don't suppose it matters but I wonder if anyone can see.

Somewhere a few blocks uptown she heard a car door slam. She walked toward the sound.

Lederer kept shaking his head. He couldn't believe the way his chase had ended.

They'd picked up the woman in the prowl car again at Grand Central Station, their own vehicle miraculously intact after going through the porn-shop window except for two busted headlights and a dented grille.

The woman was just cruising, looking for somebody to give the crunch to. Then there they were again, trying to broadside her off the road or make her over-drive herself and smash into something.

She'd over-driven herself all right.

She'd turned onto the ramp to the Port Authority parking garage at about forty miles per hour, ricocheting off half a dozen parked vehicles on the first floor and then another half-dozen on the second — and they'd thought, well, when she gets to the top we've got her. One more floor and she's got to stop.

Ladies' Night

She never did.

She never even got to the third floor. It was an incredible sight, really. She rounded a long turn. And then instead of making the next one — instead of even trying to make it — she just kept going, right into the brick wall. *And straight through it. So* that when Horgan slammed on the brakes they saw a hole in the wall like somebody'd used a cannon on it and the sound was still booming through the whole garage.

They got out of the car and went to the hole in the wall and looked down. It was a hundred feet to the sidewalk, maybe more. The car was just burning away to nothing. It had landed on top of a newsstand, magazines all around, and he could see them burning too like tiny sparks off the main circle of flame.

They drove back down and saw the National Guard units set up and moving traffic at the Lincoln Tunnel. And just after that they got the order.

The plan was for the police and the National Guard to round up and evacuate every guy in New York City. Cuff them if they had to but get them out of there. They had the city divided into sectors according to precinct, bridge and tunnel exits all closed to inbound traffic. Women were to be brought in for testing. Or else shot on sight. Your discretion.

Quite a goddamn order.

Take this one now.

Did you take her in or shoot her?

She was walking toward them up Broadway at about 69th Street, right in the middle of the street. Damned pretty girl. Body of an athlete. You could practically see right through what she was wearing.

"You want her?" said Horgan.

"Not much."

"Well I do."

Haven't you had *enough?* thought Lederer. Horgan stopped the car and slid the gearshift into park, pulled his pistol out of its holster and stepped out of the car. She was running toward him as though her life depended upon it — but they were tricky, some of them. He'd seen it happen.

He watched Horgan take his stance and bring the pistol up, take aim and fire. The girl crumbled to the pavement and lay there writhing. Horgan got back in the car.

"I'm not sure you killed her."

"Maybe not. She was moving. Not that bad a shot though. I'll do better next time. Practice practice."

"Do me a favor. Hold off on the next one. I want to get back to the station, call the wife. Okay?"

"Sure."

But Lederer could tell he didn't much care for the idea. There were always some cops who enjoyed their work a little too much and he guessed that Horgan was one of them. The man was sweating, mopping his brow. The car actually smelled of Horgan.

He'd never really liked the guy.

He settled back and wondered what in god's name he was going to say to Millie about all this, wondered until they reached the station.

Elizabeth lay in the empty street, one arm flung across the yellow line.

You had no reason, she thought, *no reason at all to do this to me.*

The chest-wound gave her no real pain. There was only a heaviness and a dull chill spreading through her body. She felt a bitter resignation.

I only wanted help, she thought. Men, cops — they were supposed to give it to you.

It was wrong to depend upon anybody.

She lay back on the pavement and listened to the sound of her breathing. She stared up at the sky. The moon was still there — pale white against the grey-blue dawn. A full moon, looking scarred and small.

What was it Tom had said? *The moon's a woman.*

But she couldn't remember why.

A car rumbled past her. The pavement trembled to her left but she hardly noticed. She watched the moon fade slowly into the brightening sky.

The car had been easy to find. It was an old '77 Chrysler lying halfway up on the curb on the northeast corner of 68th Street. Phil told him to turn away while Dan lifted the driver off the seat and set him down on the sidewalk but Andy saw him anyway. The man had hardly any head left at all.

It didn't bother him.

Nothing much bothered him now.

Not even seeing Elizabeth lying in the street as they drove by.

At least not at first.

He turned in the back seat and watched her through the rear window.

It looked like maybe she was still alive. He thought he saw her moving.

It was awful hard to kill them.

"Where are we going?" he said.

"George Washington Bridge," said Dan. "Radio says that's clear and I got people on the Jersey side."

Lizzy got smaller and smaller, disappearing, her body just a small dark spot blocks away.

"Dan?" he said. "I think that was Lizzy on the street back there. You know, she lives next door?"

Lived, he thought.

"Yeah?"

Dan looked at him. Then shook his head.

"I'm sorry, Andy. I keep saying that to you, you know? I'm sorry."

He wondered if it were possible.

That Lizzy might not . . . *be changed.*

He wanted to tell them to go back and see just in case. He guessed he really had loved Lizzy. And now to think of her just *lying* there . . .

But he'd loved his mother too. And Dan and Phil said that all of them were changed now. That was all they'd seen all night long.

He felt so all *alone.* He felt it like a physical pain squeezing at his chest. He wanted to cry. He kept seeing his mom and dad. Not like they were but like they had been. Like they were still there somehow. He was just *this close* to crying all the time.

"Couldn't we go back?" he said. "I think I saw her move. I think she's maybe alive."

He saw Dan and Phil exchange glances.

"You better forget it, Andy," said Dan. "You know how they are. You want to see her that way? Besides Phil's in pretty bad shape here."

He knew it was true. The man had lost a lot of blood and he was pale and you could hear his breathing.

So he didn't insist or anything. He just began crying. He couldn't help it. He was thinking about Lizzy and about his mom and dad, and he did it as quietly as he could, not wanting them to think of him as just a kid — and after a while he guessed he just started to accept it, felt his sadness yield to something else inside because he'd seen what his mom was like and that was how they all were, all the women.

At the bridge they stopped and the Guardsman checked their car and then waved them through.

It was over.

On the Fort Lee side a pretty big crowd had gathered behind the Guard troops as the cars came across the bridge and some of the people standing there were waving and smiling as though they were heroes or something, which was pretty stupid. And some of them were women. And this one woman who was young and pretty with long dark hair, sort of like his mom had looked in some of the old photos they'd had, leaned in the window of the Buick and smiled at him, a sympathetic smile but like she was happy for him too, and of course by then they'd already surrendered up the pistol to the Guardsman at the entrance to the bridge, which was probably all for the best Andy thought — because more than anything else in the world he'd have liked to kill her.

COVER

by Jack Ketchum

The first hardcover edition of JACK KETCHUM's third novel *COVER* published by *Gauntlet Press*. The book, about the disintegration of a Vietnam War veteran, first published by Ballantine as a paperback in 1987 has long been out of print and copies are near impossible to obtain. As with all *Gauntlet* titles, this is a definitive edition of the novel, not simply a signed limited edition.

Aside from the book itself, Neal McPheeters has provided wonderful cover art and interiors. Jack Ketchum has a long introduction discussing his research for the book, and Thomas Tessier has written a wonderfully insightful afterword. Ketchum, Tessier and McPheeters have all signed the book.

But, there's more. There's a never-before published self-portrait of the author, drawn in 1970. And, there's additional written material Jack Ketchum wrote in the late-sixties and early-seventies when the war in Vietnam was at its peak. This material, which he calls *EPHEMERA,* provides a remarkable insight into the author and has never been published before. Lastly, Ketchum has given us the mock-up drawings from Ballantine for the book they wanted to call ***Stalking Ground.*** The author's introduction discusses this in detail.

COVER comes in two states:

1000 copy numbered edition with all of the above (except the Ketchum self-portrait). One McPheeters interior illo is included in the numbered edition. Signed by Ketchum, Tessier and McPheeters. And, the free chapbook, if ordered through *Gauntlet*. Special price, mention this ad from *Ladies' Night* and get the numbered edition of *Cover* for just **$40.00 + $4.00 postage.**

52 copy leatherbound, traycased lettered edition that includes everything from the numbered edition, plus an additional McPheeters interior, additional *EPHEMERA* (never before published), Ketchum's self-portrait, a 30-minute reading from the book by the author on CD, and the free chapbook if ordered through *Gauntlet*. Special price, mention this ad from *Ladies' Night* and get the lettered edition *Cover* for just **$125.00 + $5.00 p& h.** These copies are going fast . . . a word to the wise.

SEE NEXT PAGE FOR "SPECIAL" GAUNTLET JACK KETCHUM CONTEST ⟶

To order, send check or money order to: ***Gauntlet, 309 Powell Rd., Springfield, PA 19064***
Visa/MasterCard call: ***(610) 328-5476***
Visit our website at ***www.gauntletpress.com***
SHOPPING CART AND SECURE SERVER
FOR YOUR CONVENIENCE AND PROTECTION!

SPECIAL GAUNTLET PRESS JACK KETCHUM CONTEST!

W in the original 1970 17" x 14" brown ink on white paper self-portrait by Jack Ketchum appearing in his novel *COVER!*

For the *Gauntlet* signed limited edition of *COVER*, Jack Ketchum has provided *Gauntlet* with a single original 1970 self-portrait (the same one which illustrates our CD accompanying the edition). He has donated this one-of-a-kind collectible for a special drawing which he will sign (and personalize, if the winner wishes) to one lucky winner.

10/24/71

How do you become eligible? Simply by buying the book! Purchase any copy of *COVER* between now and December 1st from *Gauntlet Press* directly and you're in the hopper.

You get Ketchum's *EPHEMERA* chapbook as well win or not. And if you order the lettered, leatherbound, traycased edition (which includes the chapbook plus *SELECTIONS*—Ketchum's own CD readings from the book), your name is entered 4 times, not once!

We'll draw the name of the winner on December 2nd, 2000. There will be NO copies or reprints of this unique collectible. You'll have the only original. Ketchum never drew this again and according to him he ("god knows") never will.

Use the *Gauntlet* secure server shopping cart to order your copy or send a check/money order to Gauntlet • 309 Powell Rd. • Springfield , PA 19064 or to pay by Visa/MC call: 610-328-5476 • Fax: 610-328-9949